LEAVE IT TO EVA

JUDI CURTIN grew up in Cork and now lives in Limerick where she is married with three children. Judi is the author of *Eva's Journey & Eva's Holiday* as well as the best-selling 'Alice & Megan' series. With Roisin Meaney, she is the author of *See If I Care*. She has also written three novels, *Sorry, Walter, From Claire to Here* and *Almost Perfect*. Her books have sold into Serbian, Portuguese, German, Russian, Lithuanian and most recently to Australia and New Zealand.

The 'Alice & Megan' series

Alice Next Door
Alice Again
Don't Ask Alice
Alice in the Middle
Bonjour Alice
Alice & Megan Forever
Alice to the Rescue
Alice & Megan's Cookbook

The 'Eva' Series

Eva's Journey
Eva's Holiday
Leave it to Eva

Other Books

See If I Care (with Roisin Meaney)

For Dan, Brian, Ellen and Annie.

Chapter One

Victoria and I stood on my front doorstep and hugged for a long time.

'I need to go or I'll miss my plane,' she said, when she finally pulled away.

'You're going to have such an amazing time in California,' I said.

'Well, it'll probably get a bit boring after a while.'

She wasn't fooling me.

'It's OK,' I said. 'I know that, unless my parents win the lottery in the morning, I'm not going to California any time soon. I don't mind though, honestly.'

Victoria gave me one of her piercing stares, and I surrendered.

'OK,' I said. 'I mind a *bit*, but I'm still happy that you can go.'

She looked doubtful, so I smiled my best smile.

'I want daily updates,' I said. 'You can contact me by text or e-mail or Facebook or even carrier pigeon if you want. All I know is, I want to hear every single detail of who you meet and what you do. That way it'll be almost like I'm there with you.'

Victoria looked at her watch. 'OMG,' she said. 'I'm in so much trouble.'

She gave me one last quick hug and then she started to run.

'I'll bring you back a present,' she called over her shoulder. 'And I hope you have a great time in Seacove too.'

'Sure,' I said, even though she couldn't hear me. 'I'll have a great time in Seacove.

It'll be a total blast.'

I blinked tears from my eyes as I went back inside. Once upon a time, my family could afford exciting holidays to places like California, but then my dad lost his job, and everything changed. It was so long since I'd seen the inside of an airport that I'd almost forgotten what they looked like.

Last year's holiday was to a tiny village called Seacove – and I *so* wasn't happy when Mum and Dad told me about it. I had sulked all the way there, certain that it was going to be a total borefest. When I got there, though, I met an amazing girl called Kate. The two of us, and our friend Lily, started a campaign to save Kate's special tree, and in the end, it turned out to be one of the best holidays of my life.

This year was totally different though. It would be nice to hang out with Kate and Lily again, but there wasn't going to be a tree to save or anything. Seacove was just going to be … Seacove, and all the time, Victoria was going to be having the time of her life in California.

It just wasn't fair!

✦ ♥ ♡

'I need to ask you a favour,' said my friend Ruby, when she called over that afternoon.

'So ask,' I said, as I sat next to her on my bed.

'Well, you know how I'm going to London soon, for a trial for a swimming scholarship?'

'Of course I know that. You've told me ten times. It's the most amazing thing ever. And I also know that you're going to get the scholarship, and be a world famous swimmer, and when you're representing Ireland in the Olympics, I'll be able to boast that I knew you back when you could barely do the doggy-paddle.'

Ruby looked embarrassed, like she always

does when she's being praised.

'Anyway,' she said, 'about the favour.'

'If you want me to lend you some clothes,' I said, 'That's no problem. I haven't got anything new lately, but I know you like my purple top, so you can have that and ...'

'It's not that kind of favour,' said Ruby. 'It's a bit bigger than that. You see, Mum was going to come to London with me, but we can't afford to stay in a hotel.'

I thought of my money box, which had about three euro in it, and hoped very much that Ruby wasn't going to ask me to lend her some money.

'So I have to stay with Jenny who's over in London on a hairdressing training course,' she said.

'That's brilliant!' I said. 'I wish I had a totally cool big sister who would invite me to stay with her in London. You're going to have such a good time.'

'It's not that simple though. Jenny lives in a second floor flat, and there isn't a lift and …'

'Oh,' I said. 'That *is* kind of a problem.'

You see Ruby's mum, Maggie, is a wheelchair-user, and for her, a second-floor flat without a lift might as well be on the moon.

'And,' continued Ruby, 'I'd be too scared to go to London on my own, so I was kind of wondering if you'd like to come with me.'

I put my hands over my mouth to stop the happy, squeaky noises that were threatening to escape. The thought of a trip to London was so amazing I hardly dared to think about it.

Then all kinds of problems presented themselves, lining up in my mind, spoiling everything.

Would Mum and Dad let me go to London with Ruby?

Could they afford to pay for me to go to London?

And what about our family holiday to Seacove?

Ruby was grinning, like she could read my mind.

'My mum has spoken to your mum and dad already,' she said. 'The swimming trials are in the middle of your trip to Seacove, but your mum and dad said it's OK for you to go away for a few days. Flights are really cheap at the moment, and since we won't be paying for a place to stay, it'll hardly cost anything, so if you want to go, just say the word and it's all sorted.'

I jumped up and hugged her.

'Of *course* I want to go. Now move over, I need to start planning what to wear.'

Chapter Two

A week later, I was in the car on the way to Seacove.

Just like last year, it was Mum and Dad and Mum's friend's son, Joey, and me. Part of me still wished I was going to California like Victoria. The closer to Seacove we got though, the more excited I was about seeing Kate and Lily again.

'You know, Kate is sooo funny,' I said when we took the last turn off the main road.

'How could we possibly know that?' said Dad sarcastically. 'You've only told us a hundred times.'

'And she's clever and brave and determined,'

said Mum turning around and smiling at me. 'We got to know her last year, remember? And Lily's a lovely girl too, so I can understand why you're looking forward to seeing them.'

I smiled back at her and tried to stop myself bouncing up and down with excitement.

As soon as we arrived at the cottage, I jumped out of the car.

'I'll help in a while,' I said, but first I'd really, really like to hang out with my friends for a bit.'

Mum and Dad laughed. 'Take your time' said Mum. 'We'll save some work for you.'

☼　♥　🦋

I walked along the familiar, brambly lane towards Kate's house. I hadn't seen her for a whole year. She didn't have a landline or a mobile phone, so our only contact had been through letters and e-mails, whenever she was allowed to use the computer at her school. School holidays had started two weeks earlier, so I hadn't heard from her since then. I was really dying to talk to her and hear what she'd been up to.

I wondered if she'd look the same.

If she'd act the same.

If we'd still be friends.

When I got to her house, it looked more run-down and deserted than I remembered. The grass was even higher than before, and ivy was creeping along the walls and over some of the windows. Brambles were stretching out from the hedges and reaching across the pathway. All the doors and windows were closed, and the curtains were drawn. At the side of the house there was a washing line, on which hung an old tracksuit of Kate's that I recognised from the year before.

I knocked on the door, and jumped as the sound of my knock echoed loudly through the house. I kind of hoped that Kate's granny, Martha, wouldn't answer the door. (Once I'd got to know Martha, I'd realised that she was really nice, but I still couldn't forget how scared of her I'd been at first.)

But it didn't matter. There was no sound of footsteps from the house, and the door remained firmly closed.

I knocked again, not sure why I felt so nervous.

What was going on?

Why wasn't Kate racing out the door, laughing and dragging me off to see a bird's nest or the place where the wild strawberries grow?

Why wasn't Martha there offering me a big plate of her special chocolate buns?

Where could they be?

Had something terrible happened to them?

Then I shook my head, suddenly angry at myself. I was just being stupid. Kate's house had always been totally run down; I'd somehow managed to forget just how bad it was, that was all. Kate and Martha had probably gone shopping or to the post office or something perfectly normal like that. They'd be back any minute, and I'd feel like a total idiot for thinking there was something wrong.

I knocked on the door a third time, and when there was no answer, I gave up and walked away.

As I walked back towards my house, Lily came along the road – I was really happy to see her after hanging around outside Kate's, making myself nervous over nothing. As soon as she got near, we hugged for ages.

When we let go, I had a chance to look at her properly. I was happy to see that she was exactly the same as she'd been the year before – pretty, and happy, and with really cool clothes.

'Any idea where Kate is today,' I asked. 'I'm dying to see her.'

The smile faded from Lily's face, and I started to feel nervous again.

'Let's sit down for a while,' she said.

The two of us sat on the wall of my house, and she began to talk.

'About a month ago, Martha got sick. She

had a problem with her heart and her doctor said she needed an operation.'

'Poor Martha,' I said, remembering Kate's badly-dressed, but very kind, granny. 'She must have been scared.'

'Yeah, I guess she was scared, but more than that, she was worried about Kate. Martha kept putting off the operation, but in the end, the doctor said she'd die if she didn't have it, so she agreed. She went into hospital just as the school holidays started.'

'And what about Kate?'

'She had to go to stay with her aunt in Cork.'

'I never knew she had an aunt in Cork.'

'Me neither.'

Lily still looked sad and kind of worried.

'But everything's OK, isn't it?' I asked. 'Martha's going to get better, and then Kate will be home again won't she?'

Lily nodded, 'I suppose so. The doctor told Martha that it will take time to recover from the operation, but that, in the end, she'll be as good as new.'

'And when's that going to be?'

'No one seems sure about that, but it might be a few months.'

'Poor Kate,' I said.

Suddenly I thought of something else.

'Kate was still e-mailing me up to two weeks ago, but she never said a thing about Martha being sick.'

'That's a bit weird,' said Lily.

'I know. Kate's last message made it sound like everything was normal.'

Lily made a face.

'Trust me, Eva, it totally wasn't.'

And that's when I knew there was something very wrong.

'What aren't you telling me?' I asked.

Lily gave a big sigh, 'Well, after you left last summer, everything was perfect. Everyone around here knew about how you and Kate had saved the tree, and Kate was like a local hero or something. There were a few articles about her in the local paper, and she was even interviewed on radio. At last people could see how clever and funny she was, and soon she had heaps of friends. It was all happy-ever-after stuff – until Martha got sick.'

'And then what happened?'

Lily shook her head. 'I'm not really sure. Kate started acting all weird again.'

'I suppose she was worried about Martha,' I said.

'Yes of course she was – I understood that, but ...... suddenly Kate stopped hanging out with me and the other girls at break times. She started to go home straight after school. She looked sulky and cross all the time. It was like an evil witch had come along and changed her back into the weird girl she used to be before.'

I had a sudden picture of the suspicious, silent girl I'd first met.

But why would Kate change like that?

'I tried to talk to her,' said Lily. 'Heaps of times. I told her I knew that Martha being sick was scary for her. I told her I'd help her – but she just pushed me away. She said that Martha was going to be fine, and that it wasn't any of my business anyway.'

'Ouch,' I said.

'Yeah, it was harsh, but I figured it wasn't really her fault. And besides, I still feel kind of guilty about how my old friend Cathy and I were mean to Kate last year, so I decided it was my turn to soak up some of her bad behaviour. And then ...' She stopped and I could see the beginnings of tears in her eyes.

'And then what?' I asked gently.

'And then the day of the holidays came along. I knew Kate would be going to Cork that evening, and even though she'd been so mean to me, I still felt sorry for her. I knew she had to be feeling scared and lonely. So I told her that my mum sometimes goes to Cork for the day on business. I asked for her aunt's address, so that I could visit her every now and then, but …'

Now tears actually spilled from Lily's eyes; she wiped them away and continued, 'But then Kate went totally ballistic. It was awful, Eva. She said I was just being pushy and nosy. She said the biggest favour I could do for her was to get out of her life forever!'

I hugged Lily.

'None of this is your fault,' I said. 'I know how stubborn and determined Kate can be.'

Lily made a face. 'I know that too,' she said. 'And I think I did my best. But still – I can't help worrying about Kate. I can't help feeling that there was something else going on – something she wouldn't tell me about.'

'Maybe it's just that Kate doesn't like her aunt in Cork,' I said. 'Neither of us had heard of her before, so I'm guessing they weren't very close. Maybe Kate was upset at having to spend time with her.'

'You're probably right. I bet it was something simple like that that had Kate acting so strangely,' said Lily, though something in her face told me she didn't believe that any more than I did.

'So do you want to go to the field to check out the tree you spent all last summer saving?' she asked then.

I shook my head. Somehow, going to Kate's special place without her seemed like a betrayal.

'No, Kate might come back to visit, and then the three of us can go together.'

So Lily and I walked down to the beach and hung out for a while.

But it didn't feel right.

Without Kate, nothing felt right at all.

Chapter Three

Next morning, Joey was up early.

'I'm going to spend the whole day playing soccer with my friends from last year,' he said as he jumped around the kitchen. 'I am so, so happy!'

The rest of us laughed, and for the millionth time I wondered how I could once have thought of Joey as just an annoying kid. I was really glad that his mum had allowed him to come on holidays with us again. Before, I used to be half-jealous of Ruby having a sister like Jenny, but now I didn't mind so much. Joey was starting to seem like the little brother I'd never had.

'I'm happy for you, Joey' said Dad. 'And I'm happy for myself too. I promised Monica I'd do heaps of repairs for her, and I can't wait to get started.'

Monica is Joey's mum, and she owns the cottage. She lets us stay there for our holidays, and in return, Dad, who's brilliant at DIY, does all the jobs that need doing.

'What about you, Eva?' said Mum. 'Have you got plans for the day?'

'Well,' I said. 'Lily's busy until lunch time, so until then …'

'You could help me here for a while,' suggested Mum, 'I've got lots of jobs to do.'

'Thanks, but no thanks,' I said. 'I'm not that bored. I'll just walk to the village with Joey.'

'Cheeky,' said Mum, but she was laughing, so I waved goodbye and went outside with Joey.

I stopped at the garden gate, and looked towards the lane that led to Kate's house.

'The village is the other way,' said Joey.

I smiled at him. 'Clever of you to know that,' I said. 'But I'd kind of like to go to Kate's place for a minute.'

'But no one's there. You told us that Martha's in hospital, and Kate's in Cork.'

'I know. It's just ....'

I didn't know how to finish. I was worried about Kate, and at the back of my mind, I knew there was some detail that I had overlooked. Some piece of the puzzle was missing, and without it I couldn't see the full picture.

'I'd just like to walk up there for a minute, that's all,' I said.

'So go. I'm going the other way. I'll see you later.'

He started to walk away, but stopped when I called his name.

'What?' he asked, fairly patiently for a nine-year-old.

Again, I didn't know what to say. This was my friend's house I was talking about. How could I explain that the thought of going there on my own was creepy and scary in ways I couldn't begin to understand?

'Just come with me. Please,' I said.

Joey grinned at me. 'OK,' he said.

I felt like hugging him, but knew he wouldn't be impressed, so I just smiled back at him.

And then, feeling slightly braver with Joey by my side, I set off once more for Kate's house.

✱ ★ ◎

Joey whistled while we walked – and even though his whistling was hopelessly out of tune, it distracted me and made me feel a small bit better.

I had the weird feeling that the brambles had grown longer overnight – almost like they were planning to wrap themselves around the house and hide it away forever.

As we stepped up to the front door, I had the horrible sensation that something – or someone

– was watching us. Joey was still whistling, but I noticed that his whistles were now quieter and less confident than before.

I knocked loudly, and wasn't surprised when no one answered.

'You know Kate's not there, so why are you knocking?' asked Joey.

I didn't really know the answer to that myself.

'Just checking,' I said vaguely.

'Let me try checking too,' said Joey, knocking even louder than I had.

Still though, once the echo of his knock had died away, the only sound was the rustling of leaves, and the distant moo of a single cow.

'No one's home,' said Joey. 'What a surprise! Can I go play with my friends now?'

I took a step backwards, and then gasped.

'That's it!' I said.

'What?' asked Joey.

'The thing that didn't make sense.'

'*You're* not making sense, Eva,' he said. 'What

are you talking about?'

'The washing line,' I said, pointing towards the side of the house.

He turned to look where I was pointing.

'What about it? It looks like an ordinary washing line to me.'

'It *is* an ordinary washing line, but yesterday there was a tracksuit hanging there, and that didn't make any sense, if no one was home.'

'But it's not there now,' said Joey.

'Exactly. A tracksuit being there was weird in the first place, but now the fact that it's gone is even weirder.'

'The mystery of the vanishing tracksuit,' said Joey. 'Someone should write a book about that. I'd love to read that.'

'Really?' I asked.

'No,' he said. 'It would be totally boring, just like hanging round this stupid garden.'

'But I don't understand what's going on,' I said.

Joey sighed, and spoke in a patient voice, like he was older and wiser than me. 'It's very simple, Eva. When Kate went away she left her tracksuit on the line by mistake, and it was windy last night so it probably blew away. I bet if you look in the field over there, you'll find it tangled up in some bushes. Mystery solved. Now I'm off. Are you coming?'

As he started to walk away, a sudden gust of wind blew a branch against a window, making a harsh squeaky sound, like fingernails on a blackboard. Even though it was a lovely sunny morning, I shivered.

Joey was already at the entrance to the lane, and I was very tempted to follow him. I took one step in his direction but then resisted.

I was being stupid. This was just Kate's house and there was nothing to be afraid of.

Or was there?

After a few minutes the sound of Joey's whistling faded away and I managed to work up the courage to walk around to the back of the house.

Dry twigs cracked under my feet, and brambles snagged on my clothes.

I felt sure that someone was following me, but when I turned around, all I could see were shadows and waving grass.

It was like a weird, creepy game – except I didn't know the rules, and I had no idea who else was playing.

The back of the house was much like the front – neglected, overgrown and empty. I forced a laugh to make myself feel better.

'You're being stupid, Eva,' I whispered. 'There's no one here. Kate's in Cork.'

I was talking to myself, which is totally weird, so I knew it was time to go.

I was just turning around to leave, when I thought I saw one of the downstairs curtains twitching … now I was really spooked …

I was getting ready to run for my life when the back door creaked open, a hand shot out, grabbed me firmly and pulled me inside. Then the door slammed shut behind me.

'Help,' I croaked weakly, as I reached for my phone and struggled to get my bearings in the warm, dark room.

Then I heard a familiar voice.

'Sorry, Eva, I didn't mean to scare you. It's only me.'

'Kate?'

'Who else were you expecting? The Wizard of Oz?'

What kind of stupid game was she playing?

Suddenly I felt cross.

'I'd say I'm glad to see you, except I can't actually see you,' I said sharply. 'Why is it so dark in here?'

'Sorry, is this better?'

I heard a click and a small light came on. It

still wasn't bright, but at least I could see Kate standing in the shadowy darkness in the corner of the room.

She hadn't changed all that much, but she had a weird expression on her face – kind of scared and defiant at the same time.

I reached for the curtains, hoping to brighten the place and make things more normal, but in a few steps, Kate had crossed the room, and pulled my hand away.

'Don't do that,' she said. 'Never, ever do that.'

Suddenly it was as if we had slipped a whole year back in time. It was like we were at the beginning of last summer again, and Kate was once more the weird girl I needed to get away from.

I took a step towards the door, and was starting to mumble an excuse for leaving, but Kate followed me. She put her arms around me and hugged me like she never wanted to let go.

'Thanks for coming, Eva,' she whispered. 'I've missed you so much.'

Chapter Four

When Kate finally released me, I looked at her for a long time. I felt dizzy, as all kinds of emotions rattled around my brain. I was confused, half-scared and angry, but still, the longer I stared at Kate, the more I began to feel sorry for her. The defiant look had faded from her face and she just looked sad.

'You're supposed to be in Cork,' I said in the end.

'Well, clearly I'm not.'

'So when did you come back?'

'I didn't come back.'

'So am I looking at your ghost, or your evil twin?'

As I said the words, I began to wonder if this really was Kate's evil twin. No matter how hard I tried, I couldn't see a single trace of the happy girl I'd known at the end of last summer.

She ignored my question.

'I didn't come back from Cork, because I never went there in the first place.'

'But Lily said—'

'I know what she said. But she was wrong.'

'And Martha?'

'Martha's in hospital. She's been there for two weeks now.'

I still didn't get it. 'If Martha's in hospital and you never went to Cork, where exactly have you been for the past two weeks?'

'Here.'

'You've been living here for the past two weeks?'

She nodded.

'All on your own?'

She nodded again. I knew she was telling

the truth, even though this truth was almost impossible for me to understand. If my mum and dad are going to leave me on my own for more than twenty minutes, they first spend half an hour warning me of all the terrible things that could go wrong. Then, while they're gone, they spend their time phoning and texting to see if I'm OK. The idea of spending two whole weeks by myself was unimaginable.

'You're only thirteen,' I said. 'You're too young to live on your own.'

Kate didn't answer.

'Isn't there anyone who could take care of you?' I asked.

Now she looked defiant again.

'I don't need taking care of,' she said fiercely. 'I'm not a baby. I can look after myself.'

'I know you can,' I said quickly. 'But that's not the way people in authority see it. They have all kinds of rules and regulations, and I can't see them letting a thirteen-year-old girl take care of herself.'

'That's what Martha said too. But who could we ask to "take care" of me?'

Kate used her fingers to mime quotation marks around the words 'take care.'

'Your aunt in Cork?' As I asked the question, something else occurred to me. 'Do you really have an aunt in Cork?'

Now Kate looked so angry, I felt half-afraid.

'Yes, I do have an aunt in Cork – her name is Isabel. We hadn't heard from her for years and years, but Martha was so desperate, she wrote to her in the end, telling her about having to go to hospital, and about me having no one to live with …'

'And?'

Kate almost spat out the words, 'Isabel sent Martha a really soppy "Get Well Soon" card, and said there wasn't anything she could do to help.'

'What a selfish cow!' I said, but Kate didn't smile.

Then I thought of something else.

'Couldn't you have asked one of the neighbours if you could stay with them for a while? They were all really nice and helpful last year, when we had the campaign to save the tree.'

'I wouldn't have minded that, but Martha would never, ever ask one of the neighbours to help us out.'

'Why?'

Kate sighed. 'Martha thought that asking Isabel to help was OK, because she was family.'

'Not very nice family,' I said.

Kate made a face, 'Totally, but anyway, in Martha's eyes, asking family for help is very different to asking neighbours.'

'I don't really see the difference.'

'It all goes back to when my dad went away. A few days after he left, the health board sent a social worker around to talk to Martha. Her name was Nicola – "Nosy Nicola", Martha used to call her.'

I giggled. 'Why?'

'She said Nicola got paid to poke her nose into other peoples' business.'

'I'm sure she was just doing her job,' I said.

'That's not the way Martha saw it. Nicola called nearly every day for weeks, and it used to drive Martha crazy. She pretended to be angry, but mostly I think she was just scared.'

'Scared of what?'

'Martha never would discuss it with me properly, but I know she was scared that Nicola would take me away from her.'

'And send you where?'

'I'm not really sure. Nicola sometimes mentioned sending me to live with a foster family, but it never happened.'

'Why?'

For the first time, Kate smiled.

'Every time Nicola called, Martha would have a huge plate of cakes ready, and she'd make Nicola eat loads of them. In the end I think that

Nicola just stayed away so that she wouldn't explode from eating too many of Martha's cherry and coconut scones.'

We both laughed and for a second I could see a faint shadow of the girl I'd known the year before.

Then Kate looked serious again. 'Anyway, ever since then, Martha's been really careful not to do anything that might bring Nicola back into our lives. So that's why she wouldn't ask any of the neighbours to help. She said it was a family problem, and it was up to the family to solve it.'

A sudden thought came to me, and even though I was afraid, I knew I had to be brave and say it.

'You could have asked your dad to help,' I said as gently as possible.

'No!' the single word cut through the warm air.

'But ...'

'Martha's never forgiven him for leaving, and

neither have I.'

'Have you heard from him lately?'

Her face softened. 'He's written once or twice, and he even sent some money a few months ago. He never did that before.'

'That's good, isn't it?'

Her face took on the distant look again.

'Too little, too late, is the way I see it. Dad probably just had a sudden pang of guilt. I know nothing has changed. I haven't seen my dad for three years now. He didn't want me when Martha was well, and he certainly won't want me now that she's sick. I might as well just forget all about him.'

This was turning into one of the hardest conversations of my life, but I knew that since I'd started, it was probably best to explore every possibility. It was like I'd started to peel an onion, and there was still one layer left. (And, like peeling an onion, I was fairly sure that this last layer was going to lead to tears.)

I took a deep breath. 'What about your mum?' I asked.

'My mum is dead.'

'But ......'

Now I was totally mixed up. When I first met Kate, she told me that her mum had gone away and that her dad had died. In the end, it turned out that her dad was alive and well and living in England. In the beginning I'd been really mad at her for lying to me. When we talked a bit more, though, I understood that Kate had been too embarrassed to admit that both her parents had abandoned her. It was stupid, but it was almost like she felt it was her fault.

'I didn't lie when I told you about my mum last year,' said Kate while I was still trying to work things out. 'I told you she went away when I was a baby, and that's true. That's all I knew, but ......'

There was a long silence, and I knew I had

to say something.

'So … what happened?'

'My mum was very messed up. After she left here, she went to live in a homeless shelter. She gave the people there a false name, and told them that she didn't have any family. And a few months after she left us, she died – and we never even knew. The people in the shelter didn't know we existed, so they didn't try to find us.'

'And?'

'Last winter, someone in an office somewhere joined up a few dots, and figured out who she was. They wrote to Martha and told her what had happened. They even sent us my mother's last belongings.'

I wanted to know, but didn't dare to ask. Then Kate told me anyway.

'Apart from her clothes, all she owned was a purse with a few coins in it, and a faded old photograph of me as a baby.'

Even in the half-dark I could see Kate's eyes

glistening with the beginnings of tears.

I hugged her. 'I am so, so sorry,' I said.

'Don't be,' she said, pulling away. 'She was never a proper mum to me.'

And then, something else occurred to me.

'All last winter, you e-mailed me every single week. How come you never mentioned this then?'

Kate put her head down.

'I didn't know how. I didn't know if it was right to feel sad about someone I'd never really known properly.'

'But she was your mum.'

Kate nodded. 'And there was something else too. You see, I loved getting your e-mails. They were so funny, and you always had such fun stuff to say about things you did with Victoria and Ella and Ruby. It didn't seem right to just blurt out, "that's all really cool, and by the way, I've just found out that my mum died twelve years ago."'

I knew how she felt, and yet I felt strangely guilty that she hadn't confided in me.

'I wish you'd told me,' I said.

She shrugged. 'I'm telling you now, aren't I?'

I still felt a bit hurt, but then Kate looked up at me and I saw that her eyes were full of tears.

She started to sob, and I hugged her again. This time she didn't pull away.

Chapter Five

After ages and ages, Kate calmed down a bit and let me go. She wiped her eyes and I wiped my wet shoulder, and we went to sit down at the kitchen table.

'Martha knows I'm living here on my own,' said Kate. 'She doesn't mind. She knows I'm sensible and she knows I'm perfectly safe. As long as no one else finds out I'm here, everything will be fine. I just need to hold out until Martha comes home again, and then we can get on with the rest of our lives.'

'But you can't hide here on your own for weeks and weeks!' I said.

Kate gave me a defiant look. 'Why not? I've managed fine for the past two weeks.'

A sudden picture rushed into my head – a picture of Kate all alone in the darkened house for day after day. But that picture was far too upsetting to me, so I pushed it away, and tried to concentrate on practical stuff.

'You'll run out of food in the end,' I said.

Kate waved towards the kitchen cupboards. 'No, I won't. I've got heaps of stuff. Martha and I stocked up before she went to hospital. Every time we went to the shop we bought a few extra things.'

I closed my eyes as I realised what different lives Kate and I were living. I tried to picture my mum, calmly coming back from the supermarket with a few extra cans of beans and packets of pasta. I tried to picture my dad, stuffing the fridge with cheese and yoghurt. I tried to hear them calmly saying to each other, 'OK. The kitchen's stocked. We can happily go off and leave our thirteen-year-old daughter on her own for a few weeks or months.'

But I couldn't picture it properly, because I knew that it would never, ever happen.

'Even so,' I said. 'You'll run out of food eventually.'

'That's why I'm so glad you're here. You can get more food for me if I need it. You'll do that for me, won't you?'

I ignored her question. Kate was my friend, and I'd do pretty much anything for her – but this was much too big and crazy for me. There were all kinds of issues that Kate didn't seem to have considered. Was it right for me to help her do something that I suspected was very, very wrong?

'What about when you have to go back to school?' I asked. 'Martha probably won't be home then. Who'll buy your school-books, and sign your homework diary? Who'll go to parent-teacher meetings and write you notes if you're sick? Who'll mind you if you *do* get sick?'

'I never get sick, and school's not for ages and ages. I'm resourceful. When the time comes, I'll think of something.'

Another horrible picture forced its way into my head. I could see Martha never getting better. I could see Kate never going back to school. I could see her living like a hermit in that small cottage. I could see her growing older and weirder and sadder as the months and years passed slowly by.

There were a million things wrong with Kate's plan.

How could I find the words to describe them all?

And if I did, what were the chances of her listening?'

She smiled brightly at me. 'So tell me, Eva, what have you been doing since your last email?'

After the conversation we'd just had, it felt totally weird talking about normal stuff, but

Kate insisted. So I told her all the things I'd done with my friends. I told her about Ruby and our planned trip to London.

She told me about all the new friends she'd made at school that year. She told me how she'd given a talk to her class about stars and planets. And for a while it felt almost normal – like we weren't huddled in a darkened room, hiding from the world.

Then I looked at my watch, squinting to read the numbers in the half-darkness.

'Sorry, but I've got to go,' I said. 'It's time for my lunch.'

Kate walked me to the door. 'Promise you won't tell anyone that you've seen me,' she said. 'No one must know I'm here. If Nicola finds out that I'm living on my own, Martha and I are in a lot of trouble. So you can't tell Lily or—'

Then I remembered something. 'Lily said you were …'

Even in the poor light, I could see Kate's face

going red, '… kind of mean to her?'

I nodded, 'Actually very mean is what it sounded like to me.'

'I feel so bad about that,' said Kate. 'When Lily heard that Martha was sick, she was extra-nice to me, but she kept asking awkward questions.'

'She was trying to be kind,' I said.

'I know that. But Lily's smart, and I knew it wouldn't take long for her to figure out the truth. So I didn't really have any choice – I had to be mean – just to make her go away. That way it was easier for everyone.'

I knew what Kate was trying to say, but it all sounded too lonely and scary to me.

'You should have trusted her. She's your friend – just like I am.'

'Lily's really nice, but she's not like you. You're different.'

I wasn't sure I liked the responsibility of being different.

I took another step towards the door.

'So anyway, you mustn't tell Lily, or your parents – or anyone at all,' said Kate. 'You have to promise, Eva.'

'I won't tell anyone,' I said. But even as the words came from my mouth, I had a horrible feeling that I shouldn't be saying them.

Surely supporting your friend's crazy plan is more stupid than loyal?

But already Kate was hugging me. 'Thank you so, so much, Eva. You're the best friend any girl could ever hope to have,' she said, making me feel really, really bad.

Kate was edging the door open, when I suddenly thought of something else.

'I called over yesterday, as soon as we arrived here. Why didn't you let me in then?'

'Because ...'

'Because?'

Then she spoke in a rush. 'I knew you were coming this weekend. I've had the date written down for months. But I'd made my mind up that I wasn't going to talk to you – I wasn't going to let you know that I was here. I'd told myself that it would be easier that way. And yesterday …'

She hesitated and I had to help her along. 'And yesterday?'

'Yesterday I saw you coming, and I so, so badly wanted to talk to you, but I managed to resist. And when I saw you walking away, I felt like crying, but still I didn't call out to you. I was sure that staying away from you was the best thing.

'So what changed?'

'Nothing. But when you came back today, I couldn't resist any more. I watched from the window, and as soon as I saw Joey going away, I knew I had to talk to you. I knew I couldn't do this without you.'

The sadness and loneliness of it all was suddenly too much for me. I gave Kate a quick hug, and then turned away before she could see the tears in my eyes.

'I'll call over tomorrow,' I said, as I stepped into the bright, airy outside world.

'I'll be here,' said Kate.

Then she closed the door and I walked slowly away.

★ ♉ ♥

'Where were you all this time?' asked Mum when I got home.

I hesitated.

I hate telling lies to Mum. Firstly, I know it's wrong, and secondly, it's like she's got magic powers that let her see right through me. Sometimes I think that when I'm not telling the truth she can see a huge banner waving over my head, saying EVA'S LYING in huge black letters.

'Oh,' I said in the end. 'I walked with Joey for a bit, and after that I just kind of hung out for a while.'

It wasn't exactly a lie, but I knew it wasn't the truth either. Luckily Mum was busy ladling out the soup, so she didn't notice anything strange.

'That's good,' she said absently. 'Now can you please call your dad and Joey for their lunch?'

☾ ♥ ☆

That night I pretended I was tired and went to bed early. Mum felt my forehead when I went to kiss her goodnight.

'Are you sick, Eva?' she asked. 'You never volunteer to go to bed early.' Then she gave me one of her look-right-through-you stares. 'Is there something going on that I should know about?' she asked.

I smiled vaguely and tried to look sick enough so she'd stop asking questions, but not so sick that she'd actually worry and think about calling a doctor.

'Oh, you know,' I said, 'I'm probably not used to the sea air yet.'

It sounded like something a demented granny would say, but it was the best I could do under pressure.

She hugged me. 'Well, goodnight then, darling, and sleep tight. And remember, Eva, you know you can talk to me and Dad about anything – anything at all.'

I escaped from her arms and ran up to my room. Usually I *could* talk to Mum and Dad about stuff, but this time, I wasn't so sure. If I mentioned one single word of what was going on, they'd be over to Kate's house within five minutes, and shortly afterwards, an army of social workers and police would appear, and Kate's dream of coping alone would be over forever. And one thing I knew for certain sure – if that happened, Kate would never, ever, ever speak to me again. She would hate me for the rest of our lives.

I climbed into bed and lay there, looking at the ceiling. Maybe I was just being selfish. After all, it wasn't really about me. Maybe falling out with Kate was what I had to do to help her. Maybe for her sake, I had to tell an adult what was going on.

And if I did that, maybe one day, in about a thousand years, she'd find it possible to forgive me.

I climbed out of bed again and went to the window. I could see Kate's house outlined against the dark sky. There were no lights on, and it looked eerie and sad. I thought of Kate all alone, inside.

Downstairs, I could hear Mum and Dad and Joey laughing. In Kate's house, the only sound would be the creak of floorboards and the scrape of branches against the windows.

Was she lonely?

Was she scared?

A draught of cold air blew in through the window and I shivered.

One more night, I thought. One more night,

and then I'll have to do something to sort this out forever.

Chapter Six

Next morning I called over to Kate's house again.

'I've got great news,' she said as she pulled me inside. 'I got a letter from Martha. She's had her operation and everything's fine.'

I'd been so caught up in the weirdness of Kate living on her own that until then, I hadn't stopped to think about how worried she must have been about Martha.

'That *is* great news,' I said. 'And if she's well enough to write letters already, I bet she'll be better in no time.'

Kate's smile faded slightly. 'Well, she didn't

exactly write the letter herself. She dictated it, and a nurse wrote it down for her.'

'But you're supposed to be in Cork.'

'And?'

'The nurse addressed the letter to here. Won't she be suspicious? What if that nurse cops on that you're home alone?'

'Martha and I thought of that.'

Kate held the first page of the letter towards me.

I read the first line – *My dear Cousin Gertrude* ...

'Who on earth is Cousin Gertrude?' I asked.

Kate grinned. 'Martha and I agreed that would be our secret code. Any letters she writes will be addressed to her devoted, but non-existent Cousin Gertrude, who just happens to live in Seacove.'

I giggled as I remembered Martha's quirky sense of humour.

'You must miss Martha,' I said.

Kate nodded. 'Of course I do, and she misses me – she's the only one of my family who cared enough not to abandon me.'

'I don't think your parents left because they didn't love you enough,' I said, but we'd had this conversation a hundred times before, and once again, I wasn't sure that Kate was listening.

'Anyway,' she said. 'I hate not being able to visit Martha now that she's so sick – but we both know that this is the way things have to be.'

I knew she was wrong. There had to be another way – only trouble was, I didn't know what that other way was. I had no real idea what happens to kids who don't have anyone to take care of them. All my experience was from TV and films, which wasn't much help. If adults found out that Kate was living alone, would she end up like Little Orphan Annie, in a home run by an evil witch, or would she end up in a wonderful family with heaps of children and pets and a mansion by the sea?

For the hundredth time, I wished I had a computer so I could look it all up on the internet. All through breakfast, I had struggled, trying to find a casual way of asking Mum and Dad about abandoned children, but I knew they wouldn't be fooled for a second, and so, I'd said nothing.

Kate led the way into the kitchen. I sat at the table, but Kate paced up and down the small room, reminding me of a caged polar bear I'd seen once at the zoo.

'This isn't right, Kate,' I said. 'You love the outdoors so much. You love walking and climbing and running. How can you bear to be locked up inside here all the time? How can you bear not walking on the beach? How can you bear not seeing Jeremy, and the Island of Dreams?'

Kate grinned at the mention of the special tree and the beautiful field that meant so much to her.

'I'm not exactly locked up *all* the time,' she said.

'What do you mean?'

Her eyes sparkled in the gloom, and for a second I could see the happy girl I'd known the year before.

'Late at night, when everyone else is in bed, I go for long walks. I go to the beach. I go to the Island of Dreams, and I climb Jeremy. I just lie there and look at the sea and the stars. Everything's so peaceful in the dark. I feel safe there. When I'm curled up on Jeremy's branches, I know that everything's going to turn out all right.'

I felt like grabbing her and shouting in her ear – *This can't turn out right. It's all too crazy and wrong. This is like something out of a movie – and I'm not sure it's a movie that's going to end well. Someone around here is going to have to sort this mess out – and I have a horrible feeling that it's going to have to be me.*

But Kate was still smiling happily, and I couldn't bring myself to say the words that would have to change that. So I tried to smile too.

Kate seemed relaxed. 'I love having a friend like you, Eva,' she said. 'You're not like everyone else.'

'Er ... what exactly do you mean by that?'

'You don't look for problems where there are none. You understand that I'm fine here on my own. I know you will never ever, ever tell on me.'

I gulped.

'I've brought you something,' I said quickly, pulling a crumpled foil package from the pocket of my hoodie.

'Mum made pancakes for breakfast, and I sneaked one when she wasn't looking. I hope you like chocolate spread and banana.'

'I totally love chocolate spread and banana,'

said Kate, taking the package from me.

So I sat down and watched her eat, and wondered how we were going to spend the rest of the morning.

☀ ◎ ✦

And so the days fell into a weird kind of pattern.

In the mornings I went over to Kate's place, and we sat around and chatted, and acted like what she was doing wasn't totally weird and scary.

One morning I was so desperate that I sneaked over Joey's Monopoly set.

'Hey,' said Kate, 'Monopoly! That should be fun.'

But after three totally boring games, I felt like flinging the whole set across the room, and one look at Kate's face made me think that she probably felt the same.

In the afternoons I hung out on the beach with Lily, and tried not to accidentally mention the fact that I'd just spent a few hours in a dark room with a girl who was supposed to be friends with both of us.

In the evenings, I played cards with Mum and Dad and Joey, jumping and trying not to go red whenever anyone mentioned Kate, or anything to do with her.

It was totally weird, and totally horrible. I never once told an actual lie to Mum and Dad and Lily, but I never told the full truth either.

And all the time, I knew I was deceiving Kate too. By going along with her crazy plan, I was pretending that what she was doing was right – even though I knew for sure that it was very, very wrong.

Every morning, I woke up and looked in the mirror. I told myself that the girl looking back at me was braver and smarter than I was. I told myself that the girl in the mirror knew what to do. The girl in the mirror knew it was right to tell Mum and Dad what was going on.

But as soon as I stepped away from the mirror, the brave, confident girl disappeared and I was stuck with the real me – who was very mixed up and confused.

And all the time, my trip to London with Ruby was getting closer and closer and I knew I had to do something – very soon.

☾　♡　★

Then one night, I was in the middle of an amazing dream about a holiday in our old house in Italy, when I heard a rattling sound. I was still half-asleep and dreaming about the cute guy who used to clean the leaves out of our swimming pool. Two years ago he'd promised to teach me how to dive backwards, but then we had to sell the house and I never saw him again.

'Hey, Alessandro, you said you'd …' I was saying, when the rattling sound came again. This time I woke up properly. I sat up and rubbed my eyes. I wasn't lying by a pool on a warm and sunny Italian afternoon. I was in bed, in Seacove and it was the middle of the night.

I jumped out of bed, went to the window and pulled back the curtain. The moon was out and I could see Kate below me in the garden. While I watched, she bent down and picked up a pebble. Then she drew her arm back, getting ready to throw it in my direction. I quickly opened the window.

'I'm awake!' I hissed. 'And if you throw any more stones, the whole village will be awake too. What do you want? Is something wrong?'

'No, nothing's wrong,' she said casually, like it was perfectly normal to be wandering around other people's gardens in the middle of the night, throwing stones at their windows.

'I'm just going for a walk, and I thought you might like to come with me.'

I only hesitated for a second. I knew Mum and Dad would not be happy about me wandering around the countryside in the middle of the night, but I'd done it a few times the year before, and it had always been kind of cool and nice.

'I'll be right there,' I said, as I closed the window.

A minute later, I'd pulled on some clothes, and sneaked out of the house.

Kate hugged me. 'It's just like old times,' she said.

☾ ★ ♡

It was a clear, warm night. We walked for ages – through the empty village and along the beach, and then we ended up where I knew we would, next to Jeremy, Kate's special tree. Kate pointed to a nearly-built house far away at the other side of the field.

'If it weren't for you that house would be right here and poor Jeremy would be firewood,' she said.

I didn't answer. Somehow, last year's problems seemed a lot less complicated than the ones Kate was facing now.

Kate spread out the old rug she had brought, and we lay down and looked at the stars. Kate was impressed that I remembered the constellations she'd shown me the year before, and then I watched carefully while she showed me some smaller ones.

After that, we lay in silence for a long time. It was very peaceful lying there, watching as the warm breeze sent occasional rustling shivers through Jeremy's leaves. It should have been totally perfect – but it wasn't.

'Kate,' I said after a while.

'What?' she said without turning her head.

'You showed me the last letter that Martha sent to Cousin Gertrude.'

'And?'

'She said she's doing well, but even so, it might be months before she's ready to come home.'

'And?

'And you know you can't stay on your own for

all that time, don't you?'

'Actually, I can.'

I ignored her. 'What are you so afraid of? You're not going to end up living on the street. You're not going to be sent to a workhouse, or to a horrible orphanage – that kind of thing doesn't happen in this country any more.'

'I know that. I'm not stupid.'

'Then what …?'

She sat up and looked at me with a fierce, cold expression on her face.

'I know exactly what will happen if I'm found living on my own.'

'What?'

'Nosy Nicola will be back on my case.'

'And?'

'And she'll act all sweet and nice, like she really cares about me.'

'Maybe she does really care about you.'

Kate ignored me. 'And before I know it, Nicola will have found me a lovely, kind foster family who will take care of me.'

'Would that be so bad?'

'How would you like it? How would you like if you were told you had to leave your home and go and live with strangers? How would you like to sleep in someone else's bed, and sit at someone else's dinner table? How would you like to be the foster kid that everyone stares at and feels sorry for?'

But I have my own family to take care of me.

I didn't say the words, but Kate seemed to know what I was thinking.

'It's never going to happen to you, so you couldn't possibly understand. Forget it, Eva, this is my problem, and I'll deal with it the way I think is best.'

I tried again. 'It would only be temporary – until Martha gets better.'

'That's what they'd say, but they might not mean it. Remember what I told you before? When Dad left, Nicola tried to convince Martha to send me to a foster family. She thought it would be a more "normal" environment for a young girl. And it took weeks of arguing and tons of coconut scones before she changed her mind.'

'But if it's just for a few weeks ......' I began.

Kate interrupted, 'Martha's afraid that once I get sent to a foster home, I could be left there forever. I might never be allowed to live with her again.'

'That *soooo* wouldn't happen,' I said, trying to sound confident, even though I had no idea if I was telling the truth or not.

And then, because I was desperate, I told a lie, 'There was a girl in my class once who was in foster care.'

'And?' Kate was trying to sound casual, but beside me her body had suddenly gone stiff and still, and I knew she was listening closely.

'Her name was ... Phoebe ... and she always seemed very happy. She said her social worker tried really hard to find her a lovely family, and if she didn't like where she was sent, she'd have been allowed to change. It would probably be the same for you.'

'Yeah,' said Kate coldly, 'It probably would. Only trouble is, it sounds like a totally fun game of pass the parcel, with me as the parcel.'

'It wouldn't be like that,' I said, 'and anyway, it sounds like Nicola knows you really well. I bet she'd find you the perfect family the first time.'

'I can save her the trouble,' said Kate. 'I've already found the perfect family – it's me and Martha. I've just got to hold out until she's better, and then everything will be fine.'

'But …'

I was running out of words and I was sorry I'd brought the whole subject up. I'd ruined our night, and it was all for nothing. No words I could say were ever going to make Kate change her mind.

'You don't have to be part of this, you know,

Eva,' said Kate in a low, fierce voice. 'You don't have to spend time with me if you don't want to. Just pretend that I really am in Cork with my loving Aunt Isabel. Then you can hang out with Lily and talk about clothes and music, like I never existed. Trust me, I'll be perfectly fine without you.'

Now I felt angry. 'Hang on a minute – you're the one who dragged me into this whole mess,' I said, as I sat up and stared at her. 'I'm involved now, whether I like it or not.'

'Well then, maybe it's time to un-involve yourself. You can walk away any time you like. I don't care.'

I felt like hitting her. 'That's not fair, Kate. I'm your friend, so I can't just walk away. I can't suddenly stop knowing what I know. I care about you, and nothing's ever going to change that.'

Kate took a deep breath, like she was getting ready to argue, then she let the breath out slowly, without saying anything.

She shuffled over to me and put her arms around me.

'Thanks, Eva,' she said.

'You know you're crazy, don't you?'

I could feel her shrugging. 'That's why you like me,' she said, and I was impressed with how brave she was being, before I felt the trickle of her tears on my shoulder.

I could feel tears coming to my eyes too. We hugged for a long time, and then we went home.

Chapter Seven

Next morning, I was really tired, but I didn't want any awkward questions from Mum and Dad, so I dragged myself out of bed, and tried not to look like someone who had been out wandering the countryside for hours in the middle of the night.

Finally breakfast was over, and I was free to escape.

'Are you going to meet Lily?' asked Mum as I headed for the door.

'Yeah, I am actually,' I said.

I *was* meeting Lily later, so it wasn't exactly a lie, but I knew I was deliberately misleading

Mum, and I felt kind of bad.

'Any sign of Kate coming to Seacove for a visit?' she asked. 'It would be lovely if you could see her before you leave for London. She's such a sweet girl, and it would be nice for you to meet up with her again.'

'Mmmm,' I said, vaguely.

'You two were great pals last year,' said Dad. 'You must miss her.'

Well, I would miss her – if I didn't see her for a few hours every single morning.

'I hate to think of Kate so far away from home,' said Mum. 'I walked past the other day, and that cottage seems so empty and sad-looking.'

I knew Mum and Dad were trying to be nice, but I felt like screaming at them to stop.

Then, as if things weren't bad enough already, Joey joined in too. 'Did the vanishing tracksuit ever show up again?' he asked.

'What's that?' asked Mum.

'Oh, nothing,' I said. 'That's just Joey trying to be funny – and it's not working.'

I glared at him, trying to give him a warning not to say any more.

Joey looked a bit hurt, but luckily he picked up my silent message.

I looked at my watch, like I had an important date. 'I'd better go,' I said. 'Can't keep my friend waiting.'

Then I ran out the door before anyone could argue.

☀ 🦋 α

I walked slowly to the back door of Kate's place, looking over my shoulder to make sure that no one had taken the notion to follow me.

As I raised my hand to tap on the door, I felt like I was saying goodbye to the outside world of sunshine and fresh air and happy people.

I felt like a suffocating cloud was getting ready to wrap itself around me.

How could I bear the stifling air inside Kate's house?

How could I live through another morning of sitting in a darkened room, jumping every time I heard the sound of people or cars going past?

How could I bear another morning of Kate desperately pretending that everything was fine, and that she wasn't bored and lonely and scared?

Suddenly I wanted to turn around and run the other way. I wanted to spend the morning on the beach, with the wind in my hair, and the sun on my face.

But how could I do that?

How could I leave Kate all on her own?

So I took a deep breath, and tapped on the door.

'Hey, Eva,' said Kate, as she let me in. 'What's new?'

'Since I saw you a couple of hours ago? Nothing.'

I realised my answer sounded a bit harsh, so

I racked my brains to think of something else to say.

'Er … later on, Dad's going to organise a mini soccer league for Joey and his friends,' I said in the end.

'That's brilliant,' said Kate so enthusiastically that I knew she had to be faking. Her life was a total mess, so how could she possibly care about Joey and his friends and a stupid soccer league?

We sat at our usual places at the kitchen table. The morning was stretching ahead of me, like a long, boring car journey to somewhere I didn't want to go anyway.

'I have an idea,' I said in the end. 'Why don't I help you to tidy your room?'

I don't usually volunteer to spend a whole morning tidying up, but I was desperate.

Kate looked hurt. 'My room is tidy already. I always keep it tidy.'

'I know,' I said. 'But, what I meant was, you could clean out your wardrobes and bookshelves, you know – do a proper clear-out.'

Kate's face was blank. 'Why?'

Because I don't think I can bear another morning of doing absolutely nothing?

Kate seemed to be waiting for an answer.

'Er … because that's what I do with Victoria and Ruby sometimes. We rearrange the furniture, and move around posters – stuff like that. It's fun.'

I knew I wasn't making it sound like much fun, but Kate didn't argue.

'Whatever,' she said, as she got up and led the way upstairs to her bedroom.

She opened the door and let me walk in first. The curtains were drawn back, and the net curtains underneath let in more light than Kate allowed downstairs. I sat on the bed and looked around. I'd only been in Kate's room a few times before, and now I remembered why. This room sooooo wasn't a fun place to hang out. It was more like a prison-cell than a young girl's bedroom. There were no posters on the walls, no jewellery on the bedside locker, and no piles of clothes on the bed and the floor.

Like Kate had said, it was perfectly neat and tidy.

And perfectly sad.

'Do you want to help me to sort out my wardrobe?' asked Kate.

What I really wanted to do was to get out of there, but since this whole thing had been my idea, I nodded, and tried to sound enthusiastic.

'Sure. Let's get started.'

Kate's wardrobe was small and shabby-looking – a bit like something you'd see in the servants' quarters when you go to visit a stately home on a school tour. As I reached for the wardrobe door, I had a sudden wonderful thought that maybe it was like the magical door to Narnia. Maybe this was the secret path to a different, better world.

As the door creaked open, though, I knew

I was wrong – it was just an ordinary, boring wardrobe.

Inside the wardrobe were a few rattly wire hangers holding up very few clothes.

There were the old tracksuits that Kate had worn when I first met her (including the one that I'd seen on the line when I first arrived in Seacove.)

There was a perfectly-ironed school uniform.

And there were the clothes that Lily and I had helped Kate to choose the summer before. I tried not to look too obvious as I gazed around the bedroom to see if there was another wardrobe somewhere else. There wasn't though – this appeared to the total of the clothes that Kate owned.

It took me about ten seconds to straighten the clothes on the hangers, and then I reached for two boxes on the floor of the wardrobe.

'Let's sort these out,' I said.

Kate seemed barely interested – like this

wasn't her room and her stuff.

'If you want,' she said.

She sat on her bed and watched as I pulled the boxes out on to the floor.

The first box was filled with schoolbooks, and was already neat and tidy.

The second box was a bit messier, and I was glad of the opportunity to do some actual tidying. I pulled everything out and piled it on the floor. Then I sat down next to it and started to work.

First I picked up a bundle of old paintings.

'What are these?' I asked.

'I did those in Junior Infants,' said Kate. 'I guess I never got around to throwing them out.'

'We're so not throwing these out,' I said. 'They're totally cute. We could hang them on the wall to brighten the place up a bit.'

Kate shrugged. 'If you want,' she said again.

I felt a sudden flash of anger. If Kate didn't care about her room, then why should I?

Then Kate turned her head, and the light from the window fell on her face. For the first time in ages, I was able to see her properly.

Her skin was pale, and grey-looking. Her eyes were dull and had deep black shadows under them. Her shoulders were hunched over, like every single problem in the world was weighing down on top of her.

I folded the paintings and put them back into the box.

'This isn't as much fun as I'd expected,' I said. 'I'll finish up quickly, and then I'll make us both a cup of hot chocolate. How does that sound?'

'Sounds great,' said Kate with a sad smile. 'Except I don't have any milk. I'm a vampire, remember? I only go out at night, when the shops are closed.'

I put my head down to hide the sudden tears that came to my eyes. This was all too sad.

'I'll go home and get some milk,' I said. 'Let me just tidy up the last few things here.'

I picked up a bundle of stuff, and an old scrapbook fell to the floor. As I picked it up, a few photographs fell out.'

'Cool,' I said. 'I love looking at old photographs. I bet you were a totally cute baby.'

Kate didn't answer, but she didn't object as I gathered up the photographs and began to look at them.

The first one was a school picture of Kate, taken when she was about ten or eleven. She was glaring at the camera, like she'd love to punch whoever was holding it. I quickly worked it out in my head – the photo must have been taken shortly after her dad left. No wonder the poor girl wasn't smiling.

I slid that picture to the back of the pile and looked at the next one – another one of Kate. There was no mistaking the curly hair and the dark eyes, but otherwise this could have been an entirely different girl. This Kate was still a baby – a happy laughing baby. She was sitting on a rug, with her arms stretched up to the sky. Standing beside her were two adults, gazing at Kate like she was the most amazing creature who had ever lived.

'Is that your—?' I began, but before I could finish the sentence, Kate was beside me, grabbing the picture from my hand and shoving it roughly into the box.

'Yes,' she said. 'You got it in one. That's my mum and dad – back when we were playing happy families. But as you know, that's all ancient history. I hope you had a good look so you can feel properly sorry for me.'

'You know I feel sorry for you,' I said.

'Well don't!' snapped Kate. 'I don't want your pity. I don't need it. I'm perfectly fine, thank you very much.'

I shoved the last few things back into the box, put the box into the wardrobe and closed the door. So much for Narnia.

I stood there, not really sure what to do next.

Kate got up and stood next to me.

'Sorry, Eva,' she said. 'I shouldn't have shouted at you.'

'That's OK.'

'And if you could get me some milk that would be great. I'm really, really fed up of eating dry cereal.'

We hugged, and I set off on my quest. When I got back with a half carton of milk, Kate pulled me inside, like I'd been gone for weeks.

'You've been ages,' she said. 'What happened?'

'Well, I got the milk from the fridge, but just as I was leaving, Mum walked in to the kitchen, so I had to make up a complicated story about wanting the milk for a stray cat I'd seen in the field behind our house.'

'Good thinking.'

'Maybe. But I was a bit too convincing.'

'When you're making up a story, there's no such thing as "too convincing".'

'That's what you think. When I finished my

story, Mum wanted to come with me, to feed the stray cat, so I took ages persuading her not to, and then she kept trying to give me food for the cat to eat, and in the end I had to practically run out of the house with Mum chasing me with scraps of meat left over from last night's dinner.'

Kate laughed. 'You're so funny, Eva!'

And you're so pretty when you relax and laugh a bit, I thought. That sounded totally weird though, so I said nothing as I put the milk on the table.

'Now let's get started,' said Kate. 'I already have the cups and spoons out, I'm DYING for a hot chocolate—'

Before she could finish the sentence, there was a loud knocking on the front door.

'OMG,' whispered Kate. 'Who on earth could that possibly be?'

Chapter Eight

Kate and I stood still for ages and ages. It was like a bizarre game of musical statues – except there was no music, and no prize for the best statue. And it wasn't any fun either.

In the end I couldn't take it any more, and took a step towards the door. I didn't get far though, as Kate reached out and pulled me back.

'Ignore it,' she whispered. 'We're not expecting anyone. Maybe whoever it is will go away. Maybe it's just—'

Before she could finish the sentence, the knocking was repeated, and this time it was even louder than before.

Kate had turned to a frozen statue again, and I knew I had to do something.

'Let me answer it,' I said. 'It's probably something stupid like a lost tourist or someone selling raffle tickets.'

'You really think so?'

I nodded. 'Sure. I'll just get rid of whoever it is, and then we can get on with making that hot chocolate.'

Kate didn't look convinced, but she didn't argue as I began to walk to the front door. Before I could get there, though, there was a loud rattling sound as the letter-box was pushed open. All of a sudden, I wasn't so sure that there was a lost tourist outside. Without thinking too much about it, I threw myself to one side to avoid being seen. Then I stood beside the door, hardly daring to breathe. I felt sure that whoever was outside would be able to hear the thumping of my heart.

'Kate?' came a voice from the letter-box.

I looked through the living-room door, and saw Kate put her finger to her lips, telling me to be quiet.

'Kate,' came the voice again, 'it's Nicola. From Child Services.'

I breathed the quietest sigh of relief I could manage. I wasn't sure I wanted to see Nicola from Child Services, but she had to be less scary than a crazed burglar or a mad, axe-wielding murderer.

'It's Nicola,' came the voice again, 'don't you remember me, Kate?'

I looked at Kate who shook her head.

'I'm here to help you, Kate,' said the voice. 'I know what's going on. I know Martha is in hospital. I know you're here on your own.'

Now Kate gave me a fierce look, and it was my turn to shake my head. I had thought about it a million times, but I'd never actually told a single person that Kate was still in Seacove.

'I know you're trying very hard to be brave and independent, Kate,' said Nicola from outside the door. 'But now it's time for you to come out and let me take care of you.'

She sounded like a nice woman, and part of me was very glad she was here. At last someone was going to talk some sense into Kate, and sort things out properly.

Clearly though, that wasn't the way Kate saw it.

She turned and raced up the stairs, two steps at a time. The letter-box was still pushed open, so I had to get down on my hands and knees, and crawl past the front door to get to the stairs. It would have been funny if it hadn't been really confusing and scary.

By the time I got to Kate's bedroom she had pulled a rucksack from under her bed, and was already stuffing it with a few clothes.

While I was still trying to think of something to say, she pulled on a jacket, and gave me a quick hug.

'You've got to help me, Eva,' she said.

'How?'

'Open the front door and talk to Nicola for a while.'

'Talk to her about what? And why?'

'I need you to distract her. Tell her I've gone for a walk or something, and that I'll be back later.'

'But what are you going to do?'

'I'm going out the back door.'

'But that's crazy!' I said. 'You haven't got anywhere to go. Kate, you should let Nicola help you – you can't look after yourself forever—'

'Actually I can,' said Kate. 'Now are you going to help me, Eva? Are you my friend or not?'

This was so unfair. I'd do anything to help my friend, but since what she wanted me to do was such a bad idea, surely the kindest thing was not to help her at all?

Kate shrugged, almost like she didn't care any more.

'I'll leave it up to you,' she said. 'You do whatever you think is best. Bye, Eva.'

I followed her as she tiptoed downstairs and into the kitchen.

'Wait,' I whispered. 'Don't leave like this. Let's talk about it for a minute.'

But Kate ignored me as she grabbed a few apples from the table and stuffed them into her rucksack.

I put my head down, and covered my face with my fingers. This was all much too mad and crazy for me.

If Kate escaped out the back door, she could end up in a lot of trouble.

I had a horrible picture of my friend, cold and hungry, sleeping rough in a field, or under a bridge somewhere.

How could I let her go?

How could I prevent her from going?

Did I dare to let Nicola in, before Kate had a chance to escape, or ......?

While I was still making up my mind, I heard Kate pulling open the back door. Seconds flew past. If this whole thing turned out badly, it was going to be my fault.

But my throat was dry and scratchy, and my feet felt like they were glued to the floor.

I felt sick as I waited for the sound of the door closing. Once the door closed, I knew I had only seconds to act.

I waited for the sound of Kate's running footsteps on the gravel outside.

But all I heard was silence.

I looked up to see Kate still standing in the doorway, and I breathed a big sigh of relief. She wasn't going to run away at all. At last she'd managed to see sense.

'Oh, Kate,' I said. 'I'm so glad—'

As I spoke, I took a step forwards and then I realised that it wasn't good sense that had made Kate stay. Because, on the back doorstep, blocking Kate's escape route, stood a very tall, very serious-looking man. He was youngish, and he was wearing jeans and a cool striped shirt. His hair was gelled up, and he had lovely blue eyes. He looked a bit like he should be on stage playing a guitar, rather than standing outside the back door of a cottage in Seacove.

For a minute no one said anything, as everyone stared at everyone else.

At last Kate found her voice.

'Who are you?' she asked rudely. 'And what are you doing in my back garden? Don't you know that trespassing is a crime?'

The man smiled, making his eyes go all crinkly and kind-looking, 'I'm guessing you're Kate?' he said. He paused for a moment to allow her to answer, but when she said nothing, he continued, 'Sorry if I gave you a fright,' he said. 'My name's Tom and I'm a trainee social worker. Nicola sent me around here to the back of the house. For some strange reason she seemed to think that you might try to run away.' I could see the muscles in Kate's neck tense up, and then he went on. 'But I can see already that you're a smart girl, and would never do anything stupid like that.'

Ha, someone ought to do him a favour and tell him that while the first part of that sentence was right, the second part was very, very wrong. Kate is very smart, but I feared that she'd do pretty much anything to get away from Nicola.

I stepped closer to Kate, and saw that her face was grim and perfectly focused. She was gazing past Tom's shoulder, towards the lane at the back of the house. She was tensed up like a cat getting ready to pounce. I'm not a mind-reader, but I've known Kate for a long time, and I knew for sure what she was thinking. I knew she was wondering if she could make a dash for the lane and outrun Tom.

Luckily he seemed to know that too. He

smiled again.

'There's something you should know, Kate,' he said.

'What?' she asked in a dull voice, like she already knew that nothing this man could say would ever, ever interest her. I could see the muscles in her legs tensing, like she was waiting for a whistle to signal that it was time for her to run.

Tom took a step closer to her, making her angle of escape even narrower than before.

'I should tell you that I was once a champion runner,' he said. 'If you run away, I'll have to run after you. You see, as I said before, I'm still a trainee. It would look very bad on my record if I lost one of my first clients. My career could be ruined forever.'

I started to smile, but stopped when I saw Kate's angry face. I put one hand on her shoulder, but she shrugged it off.

'Just go away, Eva,' she said. 'You've got what

you wanted all the time. You told on me, and now my life is ruined. I hope you feel proud of yourself.'

'I didn't …' I began, but I stopped. Kate had turned away, like she couldn't bear to look at my face.

I wasn't sure how I should feel. I was really, really sorry that my friend looked so sad, but at the same time, I couldn't help feeling relieved that at last someone else was in charge.

Just then there was the sound of footsteps and a woman came around the side of the house.

'Nicola,' said Kate, in a colder voice than this smiling, ordinary-looking woman seemed to deserve.

'Hello, Kate,' she said. 'So you *were* here all the time. My sources were right.'

Kate glared at me. 'Your source is standing right here. Why don't you give her a pat on the back – or maybe fifty euro. Do spies get rewarded for all their hard work?'

Nicola shook her head, 'This has nothing to do with your young friend, Kate. This is a very small community. You think you're invisible, but people see and hear the tiniest things.'

I thought of Kate and Martha trying to be discreet, as they stocked up their food cupboards. I thought of the vanishing tracksuit and Kate's long midnight walks.

Nicola continued, 'You'd be surprised to hear how many people care about you and are interested in your welfare.'

'Stupid busybodies with no lives of their own,' muttered Kate.

Tom quickly turned away to hide his smile, as Nicola went on, 'I have to admire your courage, Kate, but I'm afraid things are going to change now. You know you can't stay here on your own.'

'As you can see, I'm not on my own,' said Kate. 'Eva's with me.'

Nicola looked closely at me. I stood as tall and straight as I could and wondered if there was any way of convincing her that I was a very young-looking, but very responsible, twenty-five-year-old.

Probably not, as Nicola just smiled vaguely at me and then continued, 'I think we need to go down to my office to discuss what to do next,' she said. 'Come on, Kate.'

By now we had all stepped out into the back garden, and I could see Kate looking wildly around her. She looked like a gazelle in a nature programme – a gazelle surrounded by tigers. I knew she hadn't given up. She was still searching for an escape route and mentally revving up for a dash to freedom.

I don't know if Tom was reading my mind, or Kate's, but he caught her eye, and shook his head.

He was tall and fit-looking and happened to be wearing running shoes.

'Gold medal at 100 metres,' he said. 'Five years in a row.'

Kate sighed, and relaxed like a balloon deflating.

'Do you want to pack a few things?' asked Nicola kindly. 'I don't mind waiting.'

Kate pointed at the rucksack she was still carrying. 'I seem to be ready,' she said. 'I guess I must have had a premonition or something.'

Tom smiled and reached to take the rucksack from her, but she just pushed past him, flung her rucksack over her shoulder and started to walk slowly towards Nicola's car, which was parked on the road outside the house.

I realised that, only a few minutes earlier, Kate and I had been so excited about making hot chocolate that we hadn't even heard the car approach.

Kate stopped walking and hugged me.

'I owe you an apology, Eva,' she said. 'I'm sorry I thought you'd told Nicola on me. I should have known you'd never, ever do a mean thing like that.'

'Er … that's OK,' I said, feeling totally guilty.

Would I ever be brave enough to tell Kate how close I came to telling on her?

Would Kate ever understand that sometimes, telling on a person requires more courage than protecting them?

By now Kate was climbing into Nicola's car.

'It's been nice knowing you, Eva,' she said. 'Hope you have a nice life.'

Tom smiled at me. 'Things aren't all that bad,' he said. 'It's not like we're taking Kate to the other end of the earth. I can see that you're good friends, and no matter what happens, Kate will be able to see you and spend time with you.'

Kate rolled her eyes, 'Yeah, right! Maybe we'll meet again when I'm grown up, and allowed to have a mind of my own.'

She was being all defiant and brave, but her eyes were glistening, and I knew she was close to tears.

This was awful.

Clearly Nicola and Tom were nice people, and they were only doing their jobs, but how could I let them take Kate away like this?

Could anything save us now?

Chapter Nine

Then I heard a beautiful sound. It was Joey, calling out, 'Eva? What's going on here? Is everything OK?'

A second later he appeared in the laneway, all excited and out of breath.

'What are you doing here?' I asked.

'I was coming back from my soccer game, and I saw the strange car, and I heard strange voices, and I thought maybe Martha's house was being burgled. So I told your mum and dad, Eva, and they're on their way here right now. I ran ahead of them.'

'But if the house was being burgled, it would

be dangerous for you to come here on your own,' I said.

Now he looked kind of embarrassed.

'I heard your voice too, Eva, and I was afraid you were in trouble. I thought maybe I could save you.'

I looked at the skinny little boy, and hoped I'd never need him to save me from anything scarier than a kitten or a puppy.

'That's really sweet of you,' I said as I gave him a quick hug. 'But I'm not the one who's in trouble.'

As Joey pulled away, Kate climbed back out of Nicola's car and he noticed her for the first time.

'Hey, Kate,' he said, as he ran over for a hug. 'I thought you were in Cork. What are you doing here?'

'Long story,' said Kate without smiling.

Before anyone could explain further, I heard Mum and Dad's voices coming along the lane.

I had no idea what they could do to help, but at that moment, I didn't really care. Waiting for them was delaying the horrible moment of watching Kate being driven away.

So I hugged Joey again, and we waited for my parents to come to the rescue.

❀ ♥ ❀

Mum, Dad, Nicola and Tom went inside Martha's cottage and had a long talk. Outside, Joey and I sat on the grass and tried in vain to make conversation with a very silent Kate.

Much later the adults came out again. Mum came over to Kate and patted her shoulder. 'You need to go with Nicola and Tom now,' she said.

I sighed. Why had I ever thought that just because Mum and Dad were adults they could fix everything?

'Where are they taking her?' I asked.

'Nicola has set up an emergency care meeting for this afternoon,' said Dad.

'I don't like the sound of that,' I said.

'It's not as bad as it sounds,' said Mum. 'It's just to make a plan for what happens next.'

'And what is going to happen next?' I asked.

Mum smiled at me. 'We don't know for sure yet. Nicola is going to talk to Martha, though, and if it's all right with her, we're hoping that Kate can come and stay with us for—'

'That's brilliant news,' I said interrupting her. 'Did you hear that, Kate? You're going to stay with us. Who knew it could all have been this easy? You can—'

Now Mum interrupted me, 'You didn't let me finish, Eva,' she said. 'Kate will just be staying with us for a few days, until—'

'Until what?' asked Kate, who had, up to then, been acting like this whole conversation was nothing to do with her.

Nicola came over, 'Until a more permanent solution can be found, Kate. Eva's family are only here on holidays, and soon they'll be going back home. Ultimately we'd like you to stay somewhere near here, so you can still go to your own school, and see your own friends and neighbours. We want your life to go on as normally as possible.'

'But ...' Kate started to argue, but then she looked closely at the four adult faces lined up in front of her.

'I totally get it,' she said. 'You're ganging up on me. I surrender.'

Then she picked up her rucksack and climbed back into Nicola's car.

Nicola and Tom climbed in too.

'Bye, Kate,' I said as she closed the car door, but she was already looking the other way.

◎ ★ ☼

When we got back home, Joey played outside in the garden, and I had a very long, very serious talk with Mum and Dad. It sooo wasn't any fun.

Most of their sentences started with 'Eva,

darling, we know you were only trying to help your friend but …'

Mum and Dad only had one point to make – basically, they were very disappointed that I hadn't told them about Kate staying on her own. Even so, the conversation took over an hour.

I didn't bother arguing. For one thing, when Mum and Dad are agreed on something, nothing in the world will change their minds. And the other reason was even simpler – I knew for sure that they were right. I felt guilty and embarrassed that I hadn't been brave enough to get help for Kate.

Finally, after Mum and Dad had each made their single point in a hundred different ways, we all hugged.

Then we sat down in the living room and waited for Nicola to come back.

✿ ★ ❄

Hours later, after lots of trips back and forth to

Nicola's office, and lots of phone calls to Martha, and lots of interviews, and lots of signing of long, complicated-looking documents, things were sort of sorted out.

Everyone agreed that Kate could stay with my family for the few weeks that were left of our holidays. Nicola and Tom were going to use those weeks to find a local family who would then take care of Kate until Martha was well enough to come home.

Kate didn't look very happy as Nicola and Mum and Dad signed the papers.

I hugged her.

'It's the best possible plan, Kate,' I said. 'It'll all work out in the end. You'll see.'

She shook her head sadly. 'All I see is that in a few weeks time you'll be going back home to your real life, and I'll be staying here. I'll be the lonely foster-kid, relying on the charity of strangers.'

Tom patted her on the shoulder. 'Nicola's

very good at her job, Kate. She won't rest until she's found you the perfect family.'

'So she's going to miraculously cure Martha, and bring her home to me tonight?'

I felt sorry for Tom as he flinched at her sarcastic comment. I wished he could see the real Kate – the clever, funny girl I'd known the summer before. I was beginning to think that that girl was gone forever.

Nicola was putting all the forms into her briefcase, and everyone else was just standing there, looking awkward.

'So,' I said brightly to Kate. 'You're going to be moving in with us for a while. It's going to be so cool. It'll be like one great long sleepover.'

Except it wasn't.

✦　♡　☾

I often have sleepovers with Victoria, and they're always totally fun. We rent a few DVDs, Mum makes pizza, and later, when everyone else is asleep, Victoria and I sit up all night, filling our faces with popcorn and laughing about nothing.

That evening, Kate and I had the DVDs and the pizza and the popcorn.

The two of us sat up all night.

But there was no laughing at all – not even a single small giggle.

For most of the time, Kate was lying on my bed crying like her life was ruined forever.

I'm not blaming Kate. I wouldn't like to be in her situation. If my life was like hers, I'd probably lie on my bed and cry too.

But, after hours and hours of hugging her, and saying everything would turn out well in the end, I knew I wasn't helping her. I knew nothing I could say was going to make her feel the tiniest bit better.

And all the time, at the back of my mind, I had the horrible, mean, selfish thought that maybe Mum and Dad had made a huge mistake.

Next morning I woke up with a jump, half hoping that the previous day had just been a nightmare. But then I turned and saw Kate lying on the spare mattress on the floor next to my bed. Her eyes were open, and she was staring at the ceiling.

'Hey,' I said.

'Hey, what?' she said, without turning her head.

'I'm glad you're here,' I said, trying to convince myself that this was really true.

'Are you?'

'Of course I am, and aren't you glad too?'

'Why should I be?'

I sighed. She really wasn't making this easy.

'Because now you're not on your own any more. You don't have to live in that dark house all by yourself. You can eat whatever you like, and go out whenever you like. You're not a prisoner any more.'

'Did you ever think that maybe being a prisoner in your own home is better than being totally free in someone else's?'

This *sooo* wasn't the kind of conversation I usually have with friends on sleepovers, and I had no idea how to answer her. Then she gave a big long sigh.

'Forget I asked that question,' she said. 'It's no use, Eva. You'll never understand how I feel.'

'Maybe not,' I said. 'But trust me, Kate, I'm doing my best.'

And then for the first time, she turned to face me. Her eyes were red and puffy.

'I know,' she said. 'And I'm grateful, really I am. It's just that ......'

She stopped.

'Go on,' I said as gently as I could.

'It's just that, while I was on my own at home, I could pretend to myself that Martha was going to be back soon, and that everything was going to be fine. Now I have to face up to the truth. It could be months before Martha is better. You were right all the time. My stupid plan was never going to work.'

I smiled at her. 'It wasn't a stupid plan,' I said. 'It was just a small bit unrealistic.'

She smiled too, and for a few minutes, everything seemed all right.

☸ ♛ ✮

Later on, Lily called over. I met her at the door.

'Come on in,' I said. 'I've got a surprise for you.'

I led her into the living room, and grinned as I watched her reaction.

'Omigod, Kate!' she said. 'It's so good to see you. How are you? What are you doing here? Are you home on a visit? How long are you staying?'

I was really, really happy that Lily wasn't cross with Kate for being mean to her. Clearly

Kate hadn't forgotten about that though. Her face was bright red, and she looked totally embarrassed.

'Er, Lily, I'm very sorry about ... well you know ... the bad stuff I said to you ... and ...'

Lily smiled at her. 'Forget about it,' she said. 'That's all ancient history. You were upset about Martha. I'd have been the same, if I was in your position.'

Once again, I remembered why I liked Lily so much.

'So anyway,' she said. 'Now that's all sorted, Kate, are you able to stay here for the whole day?'

Kate and I looked at each other, then she nodded at me, and between the two of us, we told the story of the past few weeks.

By the time we were finished, Lily's eyes had filled with tears.

'I can't believe you were living on your own all that time, Kate,' she said. 'That's so lonely and scary and mad and brave.'

She reached out to hug Kate, and then the three of us had a big long group hug, all of us trying very hard not to cry.

If hugs could make things better, then Kate's life would have been perfect.

If.

'Look on the bright side,' I said to Kate as soon as the fuss and hugging was finished. 'Now that you've been found, it means you don't have to hide any more. We can go anywhere we like.'

Kate didn't say anything.

'So, where do you want to go?' I asked.

Kate stared at me. The excitement of telling Lily her story was wearing off already. Her eyes were dull and sad. I had the horrible feeling that if I were to offer her an all-expenses-paid trip to the moon, she'd have just shrugged and said 'whatever'.

'We could go see Jeremy,' suggested Lily.

Kate shook her head.

'Not today,' she said sadly. 'Too many memories.'

And so the three of us sat around my place, and tried to make conversation.

It was almost like being trapped all over again.

Chapter Ten

A few days later, Mum and Dad drove Kate to visit Martha in hospital. I offered to stay home to look after Joey.

'I know how much you love going to town, Eva,' said Dad. 'So it's very sweet of you to offer to stay at home.'

I smiled guiltily, feeling bad that Mum and Dad had no idea of the real reason I was staying behind.

Mum spent twenty minutes telling me what to do and what not to do while they were gone. When they finally left, I grabbed Joey and raced down the lane.

'Where are we going?' he asked, as he struggled to keep up with me.

'Kate's place,' I said. 'I have a plan – and I need you to help.'

He seemed pleased to be included and didn't say any more until we were in Kate's garden.

I took the key from the hiding place she'd shown me the year before, and headed for the front door.

'What are you doing?' asked Joey, looking worried.

'There's something I need to get from Kate's house,' I said.

'So why are you getting it now? Why don't you wait till Kate is here, so she can get it for you?'

'Er … it's kind of complicated,' I said. 'You probably wouldn't understand.'

He looked offended, so I corrected myself.

'Well, you would understand, but I don't have time to explain properly, so you're just going to have to trust me, OK?'

He didn't look very trusting. 'Isn't it against the law to go into Kate's house without her permission?' he asked.

'Sort of. Not exactly. Anyway, Joey, can we discuss the finer points some other time? For now, I need you to keep watch, and whistle loudly if you hear anyone coming. OK?'

Joey nodded doubtfully.

'Just be quick,' he said. 'When Kate and Martha aren't here, this place is scary.'

'Two minutes,' I said, and then I slipped the key into the lock, and set off on my quest.

It was kind of weird and creepy, being in Kate's house without her. Even though I'd seen her leave with my parents, I still half-expected her to jump out from behind a door, shouting 'surprise' and terrifying the life out of me.

A few minutes later, I'd got what I needed, and Joey and I went back home.

'Promise you'll never tell Mum or Dad or

Kate about what I just did,' I said.

'Sure,' said Joey cheerfully. 'I'll never tell anyone in the whole wide world – as long as you promise to play five games of Monopoly with me.'

It didn't seem fair to argue, so I played Monopoly for what felt like hundreds of years, until Mum and Dad and Kate came back to rescue me.

◁ ★ ☼

Next morning it was time to pack for my trip to London with Ruby.

Kate sat on my bed and watched as I decided what clothes to bring.

We'd stopped talking about her future.

We'd stopped talking about the foster family that Nicola still hadn't found for her.

In fact we'd pretty much stopped talking altogether.

There never seemed to be anything to say.

But in the end, the silence got too much for me.

'I'll only be gone for five days,' I said. 'I'll be back before you know it.'

Kate shrugged, like she didn't much care if I was around or not.

'I'm sorry I have to go away like this,' I said.

Kate looked at me carefully.

'Are you?' she said.

'Of course,' I answered, but I couldn't meet her eyes.

Then I knew I had to be honest.

'I'm sorry, Kate,' I said in the end. 'You're my friend, so part of me is sorry to be leaving without you, but the rest of me is really, really glad to be getting away. You're sad all the time, and I don't blame you for that, but I don't know how to help you. I don't know what to say or do to make you feel better.'

Kate gave a sad smile. 'You're the best friend I've ever had, Eva,' she said. 'No one can help me, but if anyone could, I know it would be you.'

Then she watched in silence as I put the last of my clothes into my suitcase.

As usual, I'd packed way too much stuff, and it took twenty minutes of pulling and dragging before the two of us managed to zip the suitcase closed. By then we were both hot and sweaty and giggling.

'OMG,' said Kate. 'I know what's going to happen the minute you get to London.'

'So now you're a fortune teller like Ruby's mother?' I said, laughing.

'I don't need to be a fortune teller. Anyone with half a brain can see that you've stuffed *way* too many clothes into that bag. I bet that the minute you get to London it's going to explode and crowds of posh English people will fall around laughing as your knickers and socks go flying through the air.'

'You really think that would happen?'

She shook her head. 'No, but it would be soooo funny if it did. One of your socks might end up on the queen's head, and you'd be locked up in prison forever.'

What she said probably wasn't all that funny, but I was so happy to hear Kate laughing again, that I didn't care. We both sat on my bed, and laughed until our throats hurt, and then Dad called us for lunch.

That afternoon, Mum, Joey and Kate watched as Dad loaded my case into his car for the trip to the airport.

Mum hugged me. 'Be good, Eva,' she said. 'And be careful. London is a big city.'

'I know that,' I laughed. 'I got an A in geography in my summer exams, remember?'

Mum pretended to slap me, and then she hugged me tight. When she finally let go, Joey hugged me too.

'I'll bring you back a present,' I said, suddenly realising that I was going to miss his cheeky smile.

Then Kate stepped forward for her hug.

'Will you bring me back a present too?' she asked, as she clung on to me for longer than seemed necessary.

I wondered what I could possibly bring back that would make her happy.

'Sure,' I said. 'I'll bring you something. And until I get back … look after yourself.'

Kate pulled away and faked a smile. 'You don't have to worry about me. I'm tough,' she said.

Then I jumped into the car and felt really, really bad, at how really, really good it felt to be escaping for a few days.

☀   ♥   ✳

I started to get excited as we drove towards the airport. Before Dad's business closed down, our family used to travel all around the world, but nowadays, my trips to Seacove were the most exciting parts of my life.

When we got to the check-in desk, Ruby and Maggie were already there.

Ruby hugged me. 'I'm so glad you're here,' she said.

'I'm glad you're here too,' I said. 'I've never been on a plane without my parents before.'

Ruby laughed excitedly, 'I've never been on a plane before!'

While Dad helped Ruby to load her suitcase onto the belt, Maggie pulled me aside.

'It is so very kind of you to go on this trip with Ruby, Eva,' she said. 'I don't think she'd have been brave enough to go on her own.'

I grinned. 'Trust me, I'm really looking forward to it.'

'I need to ask you one thing though,' said Maggie.

'What?'

'Can you please make sure that Ruby tries her best in the swimming trials?'

That seemed like a really stupid favour.

Ruby was going all the way to London for these trials, so why wouldn't she try her best?

But now Dad was calling me to check in so I smiled at Maggie.

'Sure,' I said. 'Just leave it to me.'

✦ ♥ ♡

Jenny met us at the airport in London, and she hugged Ruby for ages. I'm used to being an only child, but even so, I couldn't help feeling a bit jealous of how close the two sisters were. Then Ruby reached out and pulled me into their hug, and I felt a bit better.

I'd been to London with my family once before, but being with Jenny was totally different. She was a grown–up, and perfectly capable of minding Ruby and me, but she didn't act like a grown-up. She acted like a very sensible, but very fun, big sister.

Jenny didn't keep warning Ruby and me to

stay next her, or to watch out for traffic, or to zip up our jackets. It was like being real people, on a real holiday, and I was certain that we were going to have an amazing time.

I didn't care that this time we couldn't afford taxis to get around – I felt all grown up and sophisticated as the three of us got the bus to Jenny's flat. We dragged our bags up the two flights of stairs and Jenny flung open the door with a flourish.

'Home sweet home,' she said as we all trooped inside.

The flat was tiny – about the size of the smallest bedroom in the house I used to live in – but it was totally cute, with cool pictures on the wall, and a big vase of flowers on the table.

'I am sooo living in a flat like this when I grow up,' I said and Ruby and Jenny laughed.

◎　　♔　　✬

I would have been quite happy to stay in the flat

all evening, but Jenny had different plans.

'We're going out to dinner,' she said.

'Oh,' I said.

Was I going to have to spend all the money Mum and Dad had given me on the very first night?

But then Jenny smiled, 'Don't look so worried, Eva. None of us has much money. There's a restaurant near here that's always cheap enough, and at the moment they have a two for one offer.'

'Er, Jenny,' said Ruby, 'I know maths was never your best subject, but you do realise that two for one offers don't work very well for three people?'

'Cheeky!' said Jenny grinning. 'Anyway, I thought of that, and that's why I've asked my Italian friend Andrea to join us.'

How cool was it to be in London without parents, and going out to restaurants with Italian friends? I couldn't keep the smile from my face, as we changed our clothes and got ready for our big night out in London.

Jenny, Ruby and I were already at our table in the restaurant when Jenny looked up and smiled.

'Oh good,' she said. 'Here comes Andrea now.'

I looked up and was surprised to see a very tall, very handsome man walking in our direction. I looked at Jenny, puzzled.

'Didn't I mention that in Italy Andrea is a boy's name?' she asked innocently.

'OMG,' said Ruby. 'How dare you have a boyfriend and not tell me?'

Jenny's cheeks went pink, but we couldn't say any more, as Andrea was already beside us. Jenny introduced everyone, and then Andrea kissed everyone on both cheeks, and I thought I was going to faint from excitement.

I like Ruby a lot, but sometimes she's a bit too thoughtful and quiet for me. With Jenny though, it was like the two of them were a very funny, comedy double-act. After dinner, they started talking about the time their mother pretended to be a fortune-teller. I'd been right at the middle of that story, and so knew every single detail, but still, when I heard Jenny and Ruby telling it, it seemed like I was hearing it for the very first time. Andrea kept shaking his head and saying 'No? Really?' and Ruby and I kept nodding and saying, 'Yes. Absolutely.'

And then the four of us laughed so loudly that I thought we'd surely be asked to leave the restaurant.

'Know what?' said Jenny, as I wiped tears of laughter from my eyes for the hundredth time. 'I think we're going to have a totally fun few days.'

And I felt sure that she was right.

Chapter Eleven

In the morning, Jenny walked us to the bus stop around the corner from her flat.

She put money into a machine and handed Ruby and me a ticket each.

'Bus number 127 will take you to the school where the interviews are on,' she said. 'It comes every ten minutes or so. And you get off at Whitehaven Road.'

'You mean we're going on our own?' asked Ruby looking worried.

'Oh dear,' said Jenny. 'Is that a problem? I can't go with you – I've got to work this morning.'

I beamed at her. 'No problem at all. We'll be

perfectly fine, won't we, Ruby? Bye, Jenny. See you later.'

Then I grabbed Ruby's arm and pulled her onto a big red number 127 bus that had just pulled up beside us.

I felt like a real Londoner as we went upstairs and sat in the front seats. It was a lovely sunny day, and everything seemed new and fresh and exciting.

Ruby was like a child on her first ever trip outside her own house. She kept saying, 'OMG, Eva, look over there.' And then before I had time to turn my head, she'd point in the opposite direction and say, 'No, look there instead.'

I tried to be all calm and sophisticated, but in the end I couldn't resist her enthusiasm, and started to stare and point too.

Ruby was excited by the black taxis and the tall buildings and the other red buses, and when she saw two policewomen on horses I thought she was going to faint away from the excitement of it all.

'It's like being on the telly!' she said in the end, as she sat back with a happy sigh.

★   ♔   ♥

Soon we got to Whitehaven Road, and we climbed down from the bus and looked around.

'I wonder where the school is,' said Ruby. 'Jenny said it's near the bus stop.'

I grabbed her arm, and pointed, unable to speak. I was staring at an absolutely huge red-bricked building with turrets and pointy windows and flags fluttering from the roof.

'OMG,' said Ruby. 'It couldn't be. Could it?'

Then I pointed at a brass sign set into the wall – **_Whitehaven School_**. 'If this isn't the right place,' I said, 'then it's a very elaborate hoax.'

'But it's like Hogwarts!' she said.

'No it's not. It's way cooler than Hogwarts. You are so totally lucky, Ruby. Imagine! This could be your school for the next few years.'

She shrugged. 'I'm not going to get worked up about it. There are loads of people coming for these assessments, and there are only a few scholarship places. I'd probably have a better chance of winning *X-Factor*.'

'I hope not,' I said. 'I've heard you sing, and no offence, Ruby, but I don't think you'll be winning *X-Factor* any time soon.'

'Thanks a bunch,' she said, pretending to be hurt. 'Anyway, I'd better go inside and register. Have you decided what you're going to do for the day?'

'Sure,' I said. 'I'm going to go to the library.'

'The library? I don't understand.'

'You know, it's a big building full of books, and signs telling you to be quiet.'

Ruby punched me lightly on the arm. 'I know what a library is,' she said. 'I'm just wondering why you want to visit one on your holidays in London.'

'Libraries are very educational,' I said primly.

'Now you'd better go or you'll be late. See you back here at four?'

Ruby nodded, then we had a quick hug and she ran in for her interview.

✧ ♔ ☼

'So how did it go?' I asked Ruby when we met outside the school later.

'It was good – I think.'

'You think?'

Suddenly her face broke into a huge smile. 'Actually it went really, really well,' she said. 'The interviewers were tough, and they asked heaps of hard questions, but I think they were happy with my answers. I think they really "got" me.'

Ruby is usually cautious and sometimes even a bit pessimistic, so seeing her so happy and positive was amazing.

I gave her a big hug. 'So I can come and stay with you as soon as you've settled in to your incredible new life?'

'Don't go booking your flights just yet,' she said, as she hugged me back. 'I've still got fitness tests and swimming trials to go.'

But I wasn't listening. I was already planning heaps of wonderful long weekends in London.

☺   ♥   ✿

That evening, we were all invited over to Andrea's place for pasta. The food was delicious, and his three flatmates were all really nice.

After dinner, Ruby described the principal of the school.

'Her name is Mrs Armitage,' she said. 'And she is totally scary. Every time she issues an order everyone jumps – and that's just the other teachers!' When we'd stopped laughing she continued, 'She has these cold grey eyes, like sea water on a freezing day. She looked at me once, and even though I hadn't done anything wrong, I thought I was going to start crying, I was so scared. I soooo wouldn't like to get on the wrong side of her.'

'That would never happen,' said Jenny loyally. 'As soon as she sees you swimming she'll love you forever, I'm certain of it. Now we'd better get home, you need to be wide awake for your fitness tests tomorrow.'

Andrea walked us the short distance home. He and Jenny walked ahead, and Ruby and I walked behind them.

'I'm having such an amazing time,' I said. 'Thank you so much for inviting me.'

'Thank you so much for coming,' said Ruby. 'I wouldn't have dared to come without you. I hope you're not missing anything too important or exciting in Seacove.'

I hesitated. I still hadn't told Ruby about what was happening to Kate. I knew she'd be kind and sympathetic, but something made me hold back. I felt like this was her special time, and telling her about Kate's problems wouldn't be fair. So I just smiled and said, 'No. I'm not missing anything at all in Seacove.'

§ ★ ♡

The next day Ruby's fitness tests went really well.
When I met her afterwards she was flushed and
excited, and I thought she was going to float
away with happiness.

'When I came off the running track, Mrs
Armitage actually spoke to me,' she said. 'She
patted my arm and said "well done". It was
totally scary, but kind of amazing too.'

'Why wouldn't she say "well done" to you?'
I asked. 'I bet you're one of the best candidates
there.'

I half-expected Ruby to contradict me, but she
didn't. I turned and saw a slow smile spreading
across her face.

'You know, Eva, I'm beginning to think I can
do this,' she said.

'Of course you can do this,' I said, suddenly
realising that even though I'd always believed in

her, believing in herself was a totally new feeling for Ruby. I began to name items, pretending to tick them off an imaginary list, 'Passport, tickets, phone, cool clothes, more cool clothes, some—'

'What are you on about?' asked Ruby, as I knew she would.

I grinned. 'I'm planning what to pack for the first weekend I come to visit you in London,' I said.

And Ruby just smiled, like that wasn't a crazy dream – like it was really and truly going to happen.

Chapter Twelve

On the last day of the trials, though, Ruby's excitement had completely evaporated. When we walked into the hallway that morning, we noticed that someone had slipped an envelope through the letterbox.

'Oh, look,' I said. 'It's got your name on it.'

She ripped the envelope and pulled out a handmade card. She opened it and I read the caption inside – *Good Luck, Ruby. I know you can do it. Love from Andrea.*

'That is so totally sweet,' I said, but Ruby just shrugged.

'Mmmm,' she said vaguely, as she put the

card down on a shelf.

As we sat at the breakfast table, she was really uptight and nervous. She barely touched the cereal Jenny had left out for her, as she anxiously tapped her fingers on the table.

'You've got to eat,' I said. 'You need the energy – especially today.'

So she took another spoonful and spent about ten minutes chewing it.

In the end I gave up.

'Come on,' I said. 'Start getting your stuff ready, or you'll be late.'

'Oh,' she said, almost like she'd forgotten where she was supposed to be going and what time she was supposed to be there.

I had no idea what was going on, but there was no time for a lengthy discussion. Ruby watched as I packed up her swimming bag for her, and then she followed me down to the bus stop. This time we sat downstairs on the bus. Unlike the other days, Ruby seemed bored and distracted and the journey seemed to take forever.

At last we were outside the school. Ruby stood at the gate, almost like she'd been turned to stone.

'Today is the swimming test,' I said. 'You're amazing at swimming, Ruby. You could probably swim in your sleep. I don't understand why you're so nervous now.'

'The interviews and fitness tests went really well,' she said. 'And I'm fairly sure I've passed those parts of the assessment. Now it's all down to the swimming. What I do today could change my life forever.'

'And that's a good thing, isn't it?'

Her face was pale and her eyes looked huge.

'This is all too big and scary for me, Eva. I'm not sure I can do it.'

While we were talking, other girls and boys were walking past us into the school. Some of them smiled and said 'hi' to Ruby, but she barely glanced at them. She just pulled at the strap of her swimming bag and looked like she'd rather be anywhere else in the whole wide world. I had a horrible feeling that if I walked away, she might never go into the school at all.

'Would you like me to come in with you?' I said in the end.

For the first time that morning she smiled; 'Would you, Eva?'

'Sure,' I said. 'Anything for a friend.'

※ ଓ ♡

The inside of the school was amazing – all stained glass and high ceilings and squeaky polished floors. I followed Ruby down a long corridor until she stopped at a huge green door.

'This is the changing room,' she said. 'But only competitors are allowed in. You can go to the viewing gallery. I think it's up those stairs there.'

I gave her a quick hug. 'You're going to be brilliant,' I said. 'I know it.'

She didn't answer. She just pushed open the door, and for a second I could hear the sound of laughing, chatting girls, before Ruby slipped inside and the door slammed behind her.

I knew the swimming wouldn't start for a while, so I took my time going up the stairs she'd pointed at. I spent a long time looking at scary pictures of ancient people, and then I walked down another wide corridor, peeping into any rooms that had open doors.

I had just come out of a huge dining area, when I thought I heard a noise from the room next door. The door was closed, and I was busy convincing myself that I'd been imagining things, when I heard the noise again. This time there was no mistaking it. It was a woman's voice, and she didn't sound happy. 'Help,' she said in a weak, scared voice. 'Please, someone help me.'

I looked anxiously up and down the corridor, but it was completely empty. If anyone was going to help her, then it had to be me.

But what if the poor woman was being murdered or something?

How could I possibly save her all on my own?

But how could I just go away and leave her?

I tapped on the door, suddenly feeling stupid. I was probably just hearing a TV, and I was going to look like a complete idiot when I rushed into the room trying to save someone from a movie.

But a voice answered my tapping, 'Come in, quickly. Whoever you are. This is an emergency!'

I turned the big brass knob, and very slowly pushed the door open.

A small, skinny woman was crouched on top of huge wooden desk, like a bird getting ready to fly. She looked really funny, but I decided that this probably wasn't a time for laughing.

'Oh, thank goodness,' she whispered, looking at me like I was her favourite person in the world.

There was no one else in the room, and I

couldn't figure out what was going on. Maybe she was afraid of heights and couldn't get down off the desk.

But if she was afraid of heights, why would she climb up on the desk in the first place?

'Er, are you stuck up there?' I asked, as I walked towards her. 'Do you want me to help you down?'

'No,' she said, in a weird mixture of a scream and a whisper. 'Don't help me down. I'm afraid of ...' Instead of finishing the sentence, she pointed to the floor on the other side of the desk. 'It's down there,' she said. 'It's watching me, and it won't go away.'

I looked over towards the door, checking that I'd left it open. I wanted to be sure that I could make a quick escape if necessary. Then, not sure if I was being very brave or very stupid, I tiptoed ever so slowly around the desk.

As I got closer I saw that the woman was shaking. 'Don't make any sudden moves,' she said.

I could feel my heart thumping madly as I took the last step around the desk, ready to turn and run if necessary.

Then I stopped.

And I laughed.

I was getting ready to laugh for a very long time, when I realised I was being a bit mean. The woman really was terrified.

'It's a mouse,' I said. 'It's only a tiny little mouse.'

I'm not an expert on mice, but by the looks of things the poor creature was probably a baby. He was totally cute with a smooth grey coat, and bright black eyes. He'd backed himself into a corner, and was crouched there, looking just about as scared as the quivering woman on the desk.

Now the woman pointed to a brush in the corner of the room. 'Get rid of him,' she said. 'Please.'

I knew she meant me to kill the mouse, but I

couldn't do it. For one thing, he was totally cute – and for another, my summer with Kate had made the idea of killing a wild animal a very bad thing.

'Just hang on there,' I said. 'I'll be back in a sec.'

I raced around the nearby rooms and soon came back with a small wooden box, and a piece of cardboard. After a few scary minutes, I managed to get the mouse into the box, and fastened the lid shut.

The woman looked at the box like it contained a wild tiger who could escape any second, and eat her in two quick bites.

I put the box out in the corridor and went back into the room.

'You're safe now,' I said.

The woman relaxed slightly, and climbed down from the desk. She fixed her hair and stood as tall as her tiny body would let her.

'You must think I'm very foolish,' she said.

'Not at all,' I said.

She stared at me with piercing eyes, and I knew that she knew I was lying.

'It's an irrational fear,' she said. 'My brain tells me the mouse can't hurt me, but that doesn't stop me from feeling absolutely terrified.'

Suddenly I felt sorry for her. Now that she wasn't a helpless, shaking wreck any more, she looked like a woman who wasn't scared of much. I realised she was embarrassed about me seeing her like that.

Luckily I knew exactly how to make her feel better.

'My mum's totally afraid of earwigs,' I said. 'She goes completely crazy when she sees one.'

The woman smiled gratefully, like I'd given her a present. 'The mind is a funny place. I'd face a million earwigs before I could stand up to a single small mouse.'

I tried to block out a sudden picture of my mum in a room full of earwigs, as the woman walked towards the door.

'Thank you for rescuing me from the monster,' she said. 'Now I need to go. I have a job to do.'

I followed her to the door, and watched as she gingerly edged past the wooden box. As soon as she was gone, I picked up the box, and went to find a safe place to release the monster.

It was still only ten o'clock, and already it had been a very long day.

Chapter Thirteen

I made my way to the viewing gallery and found a single empty seat in the front row. All around me were doting parents and grandparents, there to support their little darlings. There was an excited, nervous buzz in the air.

At last the swimmers came out through a side door. There were boys and girls of all ages from about ten up to sixteen. Ruby looked young and lost, kind of like she had wandered into the area by mistake, and didn't really understand what was going on. Most of the swimmers were chatting and laughing together, but Ruby stood on her own looking pale and worried. Two girls in front of her waved up to their parents in the gallery, like this was just any old swim on any old day.

Ruby saw me and came over.

'I feel sick,' she said.

I leaned over the barrier and gave her a hug. 'That's just nerves,' I said. 'You'll be fine once you get into the water.'

Before she could answer, the side door opened again, and a hush spread across the room.

There were so many people milling around, at first I couldn't see who had come through the door. Ruby had a better view though.

'It's Mrs Armitage,' she said, with a note of fear in her voice.

I took a little step backwards. If this woman was half as scary as Ruby said, there was no way I wanted to meet her.

'She's coming this way,' said Ruby, looking even more nervous than before.

Then the crowds parted, and for the first time I could see the great Mrs Armitage.

I gasped. 'But that's …'

'You know her?' asked Ruby.

But before I could answer, the woman was standing in front of me.

Ruby now looked scared and embarrassed, and for a minute no one said anything. Then Ruby found her voice – or a frightened squeaky version of her voice.

'Er, Eva, this is Mrs Armitage,' she said.

Mrs Armitage looked at me with piercing eyes, and I figured this wasn't a good time to say – *but we know each other. Just a few minutes ago I rescued you from a vicious mouse.*

'Oh … mice … I mean nice to meet you,' I said.

Mrs Armitage gave me a funny look, and then she smiled, 'Mice … I mean nice to meet you too.'

Then she walked quickly to the top of the room.

'What was that all about?' asked Ruby. 'Did you notice that Mrs Armitage actually smiled at you? I didn't know she even knew how to smile.'

I grinned. 'I guess she just likes me,' I said. 'Some people do, you know.'

Ruby rolled her eyes, and then jumped to attention as Mrs Armitage blew a whistle. We had another quick hug.

'Good luck,' I said and then Ruby hurried to the edge of the pool with the other swimmers.

Mrs Armitage spoke into a microphone, explaining what was going to happen next.

'Swimmers will be put into groups of six,' she said. 'When your turn comes, you must swim four lengths – one each of front crawl, back crawl, breast stroke and butterfly.

Remember these aren't races. You're all different ages, and have different experience. We'll mostly be watching out for technique and potential. Now, first group to the blocks, and let's get started.'

The first group lined up and bent forwards, ready to dive. Behind each swimmer stood a person holding a pen and a clipboard.

At the whistle, the first six swimmers dived into the pool, and the clipboard people stepped forwards and began furiously taking notes. By the time the swimmers were hauling themselves out of the water it seemed like their whole life stories had been written down.

Ruby was in the second group. She stepped forward reluctantly, like she was facing a firing squad. Then she slowly climbed onto the starting block, like she was climbing Mount Everest. Even under her swimming goggles, her eyes looked huge and terrified.

'You can do it, Ruby,' I screamed.

Everyone around me laughed, but Ruby didn't even glance in my direction. She was only a few metres away from me, but I had a feeling she hadn't even heard my words. It was like she'd escaped to another world that didn't include me.

The whistle blew and the six swimmers dived into the water. I got totally caught up in the excitement, and jumped up and down, like I was watching the Olympic final. I'd been to one of Ruby's galas before and had watched her winning a gazillion medals. I was sure that once she got into the water, her nerves would vanish and she'd be amazing.

The swimmers swam to the surface and began to swim the front crawl. I'm no swimming expert, but by Ruby's third stroke, I knew that something was terribly wrong.

It wasn't just that she was already falling behind the other swimmers. It was that she looked like she was swimming with weights strapped to her arms and legs. Every stroke was heavy and awkward and she was splashing frantically like a scared child who'd fallen into the water by accident.

I could barely watch as she slowly and

awkwardly swam the next two lengths. By the time she turned for the last length, the other five swimmers had already finished. Ruby began her first few butterfly strokes, but by now she looked more like a drowning slug than a butterfly. The clipboard man on her lane had long since stopped writing. He was watching her with the horror of someone who can't resist looking at a car accident.

When she finally finished her length, Ruby dragged herself out of the water like her bones were made of lead.

She ignored the other swimmers who were chatting excitedly.

She ignored Mrs Armitage who was giving her a very strange look.

'Ruby!' I called, but she ignored me too.

She picked up her towel and walked slowly back towards the changing rooms.

What on earth had just happened?

Chapter Fourteen

Spectators were strictly forbidden from entering the changing rooms, but I decided it was time to ignore the rules. I glanced quickly around, making sure Mrs Armitage wasn't anywhere nearby, and then I jumped over the small fence and raced after Ruby.

There was no one else in the changing rooms. Ruby was sitting on a bench, dripping water on the beautiful tiled floor.

'Hey,' I said, sitting down beside her.

'Hey,' she said back, without looking up.

'Well?' I asked.

'Well what?'

Well, you're a totally amazing swimmer and even the worst case of nerves in the history of the world couldn't explain what just happened.

But I couldn't say that of course, so I said nothing. I sat and looked at the puddle of water that was growing at Ruby's feet.

Ruby stood up, and picked up her towel.

'Well, that was a total disaster,' she said. 'I'm going to have a shower.'

Now I couldn't stay quiet any more. 'Hang on a second, Ruby,' I said. 'You sound like you don't even care.'

'I don't.'

'But what about your dream of being a champion swimmer? What about your dream of representing Ireland at the Olympics?'

'They were just dreams. Dreams aren't meant to come true.'

I felt like punching her. 'Of course dreams are meant to come true. Didn't you ever read fairy-tales when you were small?'

'I'm not a fairy. I'm a human being – a cold wet human being, so if you don't mind—'

She was pushing past me towards the showers, but I couldn't just let her go. I grabbed her cold wet arm.

'Please, Ruby,' I said. 'Tell me what's going on. Why did you bother coming all this way, if you don't even want to succeed?'

Ruby tried to walk away, but I was still holding her back. She shivered suddenly, and then sat down.

'I never thought it was going to come to this,' she said.

'To what?'

She sighed. 'It's like I got onto a roller-coaster without thinking a whole lot where it was going to take me. But now I know, and I want to get off.'

'I don't understand.'

'You see, when my coach at home suggested applying for this scholarship, I didn't really believe that I had any hope. I didn't think I was as good as he said I was. I didn't even think I'd get the chance of coming to London for these trials.'

'But you did.'

She nodded grimly. 'Yes, I did. And then when I got here, I never thought I'd do so well in the interviews and the fitness tests, but …'

'… you did.'

She nodded again.

'And that's a good thing, isn't it?'

She didn't answer.

'Isn't that a good thing?' I repeated.

Ruby gazed at me sadly, through the droplets of water that were dripping from her fringe.

'I never thought it through properly,' she said. 'Of course coming here would be great, but …'

'But …?'

'Last night I couldn't sleep.'

'That's just nerves,' I said quickly. 'I bet most of those other kids out there felt the same.'

She shook her head. 'No, Eva, it wasn't that. Actually, I wasn't nervous at all. It's just that …… I couldn't stop thinking about Mum.' At first I didn't understand, and then Ruby went on talking. 'You see, Mum needs me. I can't leave her on her own. It wouldn't be fair.'

And then, all of a sudden, everything became clear.

Of course Ruby wanted the scholarship.

Of course she wanted to become a champion swimmer.

Of course she wanted to break records and win medals as fast as some people make friends on Facebook.

But love for her mum was holding her back.

'You deliberately swam badly, didn't you?'

She didn't answer.

'You swam badly so you wouldn't win the scholarship – so you wouldn't have to leave home.'

Again, Ruby didn't answer, but her hunched

shoulders told me all I needed to know. At last Maggie's words made sense to me.

'Make sure that Ruby tries her best.'

Maggie had guessed what was going to happen, and she had relied on me to prevent it.

I knelt on the wet floor and gazed into Ruby's eyes. 'You've made a terrible, terrible mistake,' I said.

She shook her head, sending a shower of water across the room. 'No, I haven't. If I won the scholarship and came here, Mum would miss me so much.'

'Of course she'd miss you,' I said. 'But she wants you to do well. She'd be very, very sad if she thought you gave up this wonderful opportunity because of her. She ...'

I stopped, not sure if I should tell the truth.

'She what?'

'In the airport, before we left ... she told me to make sure you did your best. She knew you'd hold back.'

'Who'd have thought it?' said Ruby without smiling. 'Madame Margarita really can tell the future.'

'Yes, this time she really could,' I said. 'And she trusted me to make sure you wouldn't do anything stupid. Can't you see, Ruby? Maggie loves you to pieces, but having you at home with her would be totally spoiled if she thought you gave up this great opportunity for her.'

'She's my mum. She's always taken care of me. So how could I turn my back and leave her on her own?'

'Maggie will be fine. She's well able to look after herself, and if she needs help, she's got heaps of friends, and Jenny will be back home in a few months time.'

Ruby shrugged. 'Even if you're right—'

'I am right!'

'Maybe – but it's too late now. I swam like an elephant on tranquillisers. I've thrown away my chance, and I won't get another one.

'Do you *want* another chance?'

Ruby didn't say anything, but I took the sudden sparkle in her eyes as her answer.

'Then leave it to Eva!' I said as I raced back to the pool area.

⚹ 🌱 ♡

Mrs Armitage was barking instructions as she lined up a group of swimmers.

As soon as the swimmers had dived into the water, I took my opportunity and raced over.

'You again?' she said.

'I need to talk to you, Mrs Armitage,' I said. 'It's urgent.'

'I'm ever so slightly busy,' she said sarcastically, but then she smiled. 'However, I think I might be a little in your debt. So talk to me.'

'It's about my friend Ruby – Ruby Miller.'

Mrs Armitage thought for a second, and then she started to flip through the pages on her clipboard.

'Oh, yes,' she said in the end. 'Ruby Miller – her coach recommended that girl so highly, and she did very well on her first two days here. I thought she had incredible potential, but I was wrong. It just goes to show that there are no certainties in this business. I'm sorry about your friend but …'

She was already walking away, and I knew I had to do something.

'Please,' I said. 'I'm begging you to listen to me. If you knew what I know, you'd definitely give Ruby another chance.'

'Well now you have me interested,' she said. 'Just wait here while I watch this group of swimmers. When they finish their trial, I'll give you one minute to convince me.'

One minute didn't seem like a whole lot of time to change someone's life.

I stood to one side and furiously racked my brains for the right words to convince Mrs Armitage. This was a huge responsibility, and I wasn't sure if I was ready for it.

Ruby's whole future was in my hands.

If I could think of the right words, maybe the scholarship could still be hers.

And at the back of my mind was a horrible thought – in years to come, when Maggie was missing her daughter, would she thank me or hate me? But I'd made my decision …

Much too soon, the swimmers were hauling themselves out of the water, and Mrs Armitage was walking towards me. She stopped in front of me and folded her arms.

'One minute, remember,' she said. 'So make it good.'

One minute is very short so I didn't waste any of it on breathing, and all my words came out in a rush.

'Ruby's coach was right – she is an amazing swimmer – like a fish or a dolphin or – well like anything that swims amazingly – but she didn't swim her best this morning because –

well, because she didn't want to – well, she did want to – but she didn't want to *too* – if that makes any sense – you see she's afraid her mum couldn't manage on her own – she's disabled you see – but she's much more independent than Ruby realises – so anyway, Ruby deliberately failed the swimming tests – but her mum had warned me about that – and now even though Ruby's probably the best swimmer in the whole place – you're going to send her away – and that would be such a big mistake and – if she got another chance – I know you wouldn't be sorry – she'd show you how well she can swim and please, please, please ……'

Finally I ran out of breath. I stood there gasping like a swimmer who'd just swum four lengths of the pool. As I tried to catch my breath to say more, I felt like a contestant on a quiz show, and the precious seconds were ticking by much too fast.

Mrs Armitage said nothing. She consulted

her clipboard, flipping backwards and forwards between the pages.

I wondered if she'd heard me at all.

Had she forgotten that I was even there?

Then she spoke without even looking up.

'A girl has been taken ill, so there's a gap in the second-next trial.'

I wasn't sure I understood. 'You're giving Ruby another chance?'

'Yes,' she said. 'So go and tell her to get ready.'

I resisted the urge to hug her. Even though we were practically best friends by now, she really didn't look like the huggy type.

As I turned to go, Mrs Armitage put one hand on my shoulder and spoke again.

'If Ruby is as good at swimming as she is at choosing friends, then I think she'll go a long way.'

★ ✿ ❤

When I got back to the changing room, Ruby

was sitting in the same place, shivering.

'You're on,' I said. 'Mrs Armitage is giving you another chance. Get yourself ready.'

Ruby grabbed her swimming hat and goggles from the bench beside her and jumped up beaming. Then her smile vanished.

'I've been sitting here for too long. I think I might be too cold to swim,' she said.

There was no way I was letting her give up now.

'Forget it,' I said, as I pushed her towards the door to the pool. 'Just think of the amazing sun holiday you're going to bring me on when you're rich and famous. That should make you warm. Now get into the water and swim like your life depends on it.'

A few minutes later, Ruby dived into the pool, and she swam like there were hundreds of sharks snapping at her heels. She raced up and down the pool, faster than everyone else. I jumped to my feet and screamed her name over and over again. Then it was like the last scene of a soppy film, as everyone in the crowd stood up too and stamped and whistled and shouted.

When Ruby got out of the water, and realised that all the cheering was for her, she went bright red. One more time I broke the rules and jumped over the fence. I raced over to Ruby and hugged her, not caring that my best clothes were getting soaked all over again.

Mrs Armitage came over and suddenly I didn't care that she wasn't a huggy kind of woman. I threw my arms around her and squeezed her tight, making the crowd scream wildly.

Mrs Armitage pulled away, smiling weakly. She patted Ruby on the back.

'What an amazing transformation,' she said. 'I think it's safe to say that we're going to be seeing a lot of Ruby Miller over the next couple of years.'

'So I'm getting a scholarship?' said Ruby, going even redder than before.

'We just need to sort out the paperwork, and we'll send your family all the necessary documents next week. But basically, yes, you're in.'

Then Ruby shrieked and grabbed me and hugged me one more time, and even though my best top was now forever ruined from chlorine and water, I didn't care at all.

Chapter Fifteen

The next morning we got up really early.

'It's your last day in London,' said Jenny, 'so I've taken the day off. Now what are we going to do?'

For a minute I thought of all the things I did with my parents when we visited London the last time, back when we had lots of money.

But we couldn't afford any of this now, and besides, I had another idea.

'There is one thing. I'd kind of like to …' I began, but then stopped. My idea was a bit crazy, and I wasn't sure how to continue.

Jenny and Ruby stared at me, and I could feel my face going red.

'This has got something to do with your secretive trips to the library, hasn't it?' asked Ruby.

I nodded, and then I took a deep breath and told them the whole story.

'So basically, you're trying to track down Kate's dad and ask him to take care of her?' said Jenny, when I'd finished. 'That's really kind of you, Eva, but isn't it a bit risky? What if he says "no"? Won't Kate be devastated?'

I sighed. 'I'm not an idiot. I haven't told Kate anything about my plan.'

'But he's been gone for years, hasn't he?' said Ruby gently.

I nodded. 'Yes. And I know I'm probably wasting my time. But for Kate's sake, I have to give it a try. And if her dad doesn't want to help her, well at least Kate will never know what happened.'

'Right,' said Jenny. 'Tell us what you've discovered so far.'

I sighed.

'Not a whole lot. I've spent hours on the internet, but I haven't made any progress at all. Why couldn't Kate's dad have a helpful name like Nathaniel Chippenbottom or something? Do you have any idea how many Patrick Ryan's there are in London?'

'How many?' asked Ruby.

I shrugged. 'I can't say for sure, but I know it's a lot – hundreds.'

'Well, that's not going to be a help,' said Jenny. 'It's a pity you don't have a photograph of him.'

I grinned. 'Actually I do.'

I ran and got the photo of Kate's dad that I had 'borrowed' from her house the day I'd sneaked in there.

'He looks nice,' said Ruby, as she examined the photo. 'He's got a friendly smile.'

'I know,' I said. 'And Kate has lots of happy

memories of him. But if he's so nice, why did he vanish from her life like that?'

'You never know what's going on in someone else's life,' said Jenny. 'Maybe he had problems that Kate never knew about.'

'Anyway,' said Ruby. 'None of this is helping us to find him. We have his name and a photograph, but he's not a lost dog. We can hardly stick up "missing" posters all over London. Do you know anything else about him, Eva?'

I sighed. 'Hardly anything. Kate never says a whole lot about him.'

'Do you know what he does for a living?' asked Jenny.

I shook my head. 'No idea, I'm afraid. When Kate does mention him she usually just talks about all the time they spent together in their special field.'

'When I met Kate last year, she told me that her dad was big into nature,' said Ruby suddenly.

'Yeah, but loads of people are big into nature,'

I said. 'We can hardly wander around every park in London, hoping to find Kate's dad hugging a tree, or reciting a love poem to a rose bush.'

'What else was he interested in?' asked Jenny, giggling.

And then it came to me. 'Stars,' I said. 'He was really, really into stars.'

'Football stars? Movie stars?' asked Jenny.

'Not that kind of star. I meant real stars – the ones in the sky. Kate knows all about them, because her father was kind of obsessed with them.'

'That's where we start then,' said Jenny. 'Get your coats, girls, we're going on a mission.'

I jumped up quickly and hugged Jenny. 'What was that for?' she asked, looking surprised and pleased.

Because you're so cool and funny?

Because now that you're involved, I think this plan might actually work?

Because instead of finding a hundred reasons not

to do this you've just decided to get stuck in?

Because I would so much love to have a brilliant big sister like you?

But all those things would have sounded much too weird and embarrassing, so I said, 'Just because. Now let's go. We can't afford to waste any time.'

☾　★　✧

An hour later we were standing outside the head office of Astronomy UK.

'You know they're going to think we're totally crazy?' said Ruby.

'And we care because?' said Jenny pushing open the door. 'Now remember, we don't need to give away too many details. We'll just say we're looking for this man. We won't say why, and hopefully they won't ask.'

The friendly receptionist didn't recognise Patrick from the photograph, but she put his name through the computer, and I was very hopeful for about three seconds, until she said, 'Sorry, girls. There's no Patrick Ryan on our membership list.'

'Oh,' I said so sadly that she smiled at me.

'Don't worry. That just means that he's not signed up. Lots of people come to our meetings without ever formally registering. Why don't you come along to our next gathering and you might see him then?'

'When is your next gathering?' asked Jenny.

The woman consulted a calendar. 'Six weeks time.'

I sighed. We barely had six hours left.

We thanked the woman and were walking away when she called us back. 'You know there are three smaller, local astronomy groups in London. Maybe your friend is part of one of them?'

I felt like kissing her as she wrote down the names and contact details of the leaders of the three smaller groups.

'I feel like a proper detective,' said Ruby as we set off to track down the first person on the list. 'Who'd have thought that searching for a lost person could be so much fun?'

Chapter Sixteen

Three hours later, the search didn't seem like so much fun any more. We had made no progress at all, and we were getting tired. I wondered how tv detectives managed to solve their cases in an hour – with ad-breaks.

It had taken us ages to find the first person on the list. When we did find him, he turned out to be really mean and grumpy and he didn't know anything about Kate's dad either.

When we finally got to the apartment of the second person, her flatmate told us that she wasn't there.

'Will she be back soon?' I asked hopefully.

The flatmate shook her head. 'Sorry. She's gone on an astronomy tour of South America. She won't be back for months. I don't suppose you'd like to sublet her room? I can't afford the rent on my own.'

We assured her that we weren't looking for a home, and then left, feeling totally fed up.

By the time we knocked on the door of the third group leader, I didn't dare to feel hopeful any more. I felt that I was messing up our last day in London, and it was all going to be for nothing.

The man who answered the door was suspicious when we asked him if he knew Patrick Ryan.

'I don't know him,' he said. 'And even if I did, I'm not sure I'd tell you. Does he owe you money or something?'

'No,' said Ruby quickly. 'It's nothing like that. Patrick is an old friend, and we want to give him some good news about his family.'

I wasn't sure what part of *Your mother is sick and it's looking like your daughter will have to go into care* was good news.

Still, I couldn't worry about details like that now. This was our last chance to help Kate, and I had to make the most of it. I pulled out the photograph.

'This is him,' I said. 'Has he ever been to any of your meetings?'

The man looked at the photograph for a long time. 'He does look kind of familiar, but I don't know who he is. You should find Peggy. She's a regular at our meetings, and she knows everything about everyone. If anyone knows your friend, she will. She lives down on Bridge Street, right next to the flower shop.'

I wasn't sure if he was really trying to be helpful, or if he just wanted to get rid of us, but all of a sudden I didn't care.

Before we'd finished thanking him, he had closed the door in our faces.

'Charming,' said Ruby, as we walked away.

☾　✦　☾

When we got to Peggy's house, the front door was opened by a thin woman with neat grey hair. Before we even had time to explain what we wanted, she had invited us in for tea. Tea sounded nice, but Jenny refused.

'Thanks very much,' she said. 'But we're just here to see if you know this man.'

Peggy smiled when I showed her the photograph. 'I don't think this was taken any time recently,' she said. 'But I definitely know that man. He's a regular at our monthly astronomy meetings. He's not very talkative, is he?'

'I wouldn't know,' I said, before Jenny poked me in the ribs. 'I mean, I know,' I said quickly.

'Anyway,' said Jenny. 'Do you know where he lives?'

Peggy shook her head. 'Like I said, he doesn't

say much. But I can give him a message when I see him if you like. We have a meeting in three weeks time and I'm sure he'll be there.'

'Thanks, but that's too late for us,' I said as we turned to go.

We'd reached a dead end. It was time to face up to the fact that there was nothing I could do to help Kate.

Just then a small black dog came running from the back of the house.

'My little baby,' said Peggy scooping him up. 'Come and meet the nice girls.'

I had the awful feeling that the woman was lonely, and didn't want us to leave.

'Isn't he a darling?' she asked, grabbing one of his skinny paws and waving it at us.

'He's lovely,' said Ruby politely, even though he was the ugliest, scrawniest dog I'd ever seen.

'What's his name?' I asked, jumping backwards as the dog puffed a stinky waft of dog-breath into my face.

'This is Edgar,' said Peggy. 'And goodness gracious, why didn't I remember this before?'

'Remember what?' I asked, bracing myself for a long boring story about her darling dog.

'That man you're looking for – Patrick,' said Peggy. 'One day while we were waiting for the astronomy meeting to start, I was telling him about Edgar's toenail operation, and Patrick didn't seem very interested, I have to say, but when I was finished he did mention that "Edgar" was an unusual name for a dog, and I told him that Edgar was called after the writer Edgar Allen Poe, because my late father was a big fan of his and ……'

She rattled on for a long time, and even though I felt sorry for the lonely old lady, I had a feeling that she was just wasting our time. But then, amazingly, she finally got to the point.

'…… and then Patrick said that he lived on a street with the same name as my dog.'

'So he lives on Edgar Street?' said Jenny. 'Do

you happen to know where that is?'

'Actually, I do,' said Peggy. 'My aunt Julia used to work near there, and sometimes when I was a little girl, I went to her office on my way home from school. Julia was a nice old lady, but a bit disorganised. One day she …..'

What felt like hours later, we'd got directions to Edgar Street, and we thanked Peggy and set off on the next step of our journey.

Luckily, Edgar Street was small, with only a few houses on it. The woman in the first house was very helpful when we showed her the photograph.

'I don't know his name,' she said. 'But he lives just across there, in the house with the blue door.'

'I can't believe we've actually done this,' said Ruby as we crossed the road. 'Don't you feel proud and clever and grown-up, Eva?'

I shook my head. I didn't feel any of those things – I just felt sick and nervous.

'What are we going to do if he's not there?' asked Jenny.

'What are we going to do if he *is* there?' I asked.

'What do you mean?' asked Jenny.

I stopped on the footpath, and sighed. 'This was a totally stupid idea. I don't know why we've bothered. Patrick knows where Kate is. If he cared about her, he'd have come home years ago. Nothing we say will make any difference to him. I'm sorry, Ruby and Jenny. I've messed up your day for nothing.'

'Hey,' said Jenny putting her arm around me. 'This isn't like you, Eva. You helped Mum and Ruby last year, and you helped Kate too. I know you're not going to give up now – not when we're so close.'

I wasn't sure she was right, but before I could answer her, she was marching up the driveway and knocking on the door.

'Come on, Eva,' she said. 'Don't let me do this all on my own.'

So Ruby and I ran up the driveway and arrived just as the door was pulled open. I was bracing myself for my first look at Kate's long-lost father and was totally surprised to see a pretty woman, with long brown hair, and kind eyes. She was wearing jeans and a big baggy jumper, and in her arms was a totally cute, curly-haired baby.

The woman smiled and spoke in an American accent, 'Hello girls,' she said. 'What can I do for you all?'

I was embarrassed.

'Sorry,' I said. 'We didn't mean to bother you. We were looking for someone, but I think we've come to the wrong place.'

I was turning to walk away, when Ruby grabbed my arm.

'Show her the photograph, Eva,' she said.

'Yes, do show me the photograph,' said the

woman. 'If your friend lives around here, maybe I can help you to find them.'

He's no friend of ours, I felt like shouting.

I was cross now. I was wasting my time, and ruining the last day of Ruby's trip.

But everyone was staring at me and waiting, so I pulled the photograph from its envelope and held it towards the woman. The baby grabbed for it, and the woman pulled it away from him.

'No, Simon,' she said. 'That's not your dinner.' She looked at the photograph and gave a big laugh. 'Oh my!' she said. 'Look at that, Simon. It's your daddy!'

I could feel the blood draining from my face. 'But it can't be,' I said.

The woman laughed again. 'I've never seen him with such a bad haircut, but there's no mistaking that smile. That's my husband, Patrick.'

Chapter Seventeen

Ruby, Jenny and I stood on the doorstep like we'd been turned to cold, stone statues of ourselves.

This didn't make any sense.

How could Patrick be married?

How could he have a wife and baby?

How could he be playing happy families here in London, while Kate, his real family, was all alone in Ireland?

Just then a door opened at the back of the house, and a man walked along the corridor towards us.

His hair and his face had both got thinner,

but even so, I was certain that I was looking at Kate's dad.

He was smiling at us, like he was perfectly innocent, like he'd done nothing wrong in his whole life.

'What's going on out here, Zoe?' he said. 'I've made Simon's tea, and it'll be going cold.'

While he spoke, he gently stroked the baby's hair, and the baby gazed at him adoringly.

Suddenly I felt like screaming.

How dare he love this baby, when right now, Kate was probably lying on my bed sobbing her heart out because she had to go and live with strangers?

I grabbed the photograph from Zoe's hand and shoved it into my pocket, not caring that I was crumpling it up and ruining it.

'There's something I'd like to tell you,' I said to Patrick.

I wasn't sure what exactly I was going to say, but I knew it wasn't going to be nice.

Jenny must have guessed that I wasn't going to be very diplomatic. She smiled at Zoe.

'Do you think you could excuse us for just a minute?' she said. 'There's something we need to say to Patrick.' Zoe gave us a funny look, but she didn't move. 'It's about astronomy,' said Jenny quickly. 'My sister and her friend want to interview amateur astronomers for their school magazine. You could listen if you like, but you'd probably be totally bored, and we'd feel bad if the baby's tea got cold.'

Zoe started to turn away, but then she turned back again. 'So how come you've got a photograph of Patrick?' she asked.

There was a long silence.

I looked at Ruby and Ruby looked at Jenny, and the baby laughed like this was all very funny.

'It's kind of a long story,' I said. 'You see ....'

I stopped and Jenny must have guessed that I had no idea what to say next.

'You see, my third cousin, Seamus, was in

school with Patrick, years ago, in Ireland,' she said. 'And when we said we were coming here, Seamus found this photo in an old album, and he said it would be funny to bring it along. So we did.'

'Seamus who?' asked Patrick.

Jenny smiled at him, 'Seamus Murphy. But you might not remember him. It was a long time ago, and cousin Seamus is a forgettable kind of guy.'

By now Zoe must have been tired of talking about long-lost friends called Seamus. 'I'll go in back and feed Simon,' she said. 'You guys take all the time you need.'

Then she went into a room at the back of the house, closing the door behind her.

♥　✿　★

For a minute no one said anything. Patrick stood there calmly, with his arms folded. He was probably expecting some not-very-exciting questions about galaxies and telescopes. Clearly he had *nooooo* idea what was coming next. I'd have felt sorry for him – except that I was angrier than I had ever been in my entire life.

I was afraid to open my mouth. I felt like there was a volcano simmering inside me. I was sure that if I said a single word to Patrick, it would trigger an explosion that I could never manage to control.

Then I remembered the other photograph in the envelope. It was a really nice one that I'd taken of Kate next to her special tree the summer before. I took out the photograph and handed it to Patrick. He looked at it for a long, long time. Then he covered his face with his hands.

When at last he spoke, his voice was totally weird – all hoarse and croaky.

'That's Kate,' he said. 'My Kate.'

'Yes,' I said. 'You got it in one. That's Kate – your daughter. I'm surprised you even remember her name.'

'But who are you?' he asked. 'Why are you here? Has something happened? Is Kate all right?'

Now I couldn't hold back my anger any more. 'How could she possibly be all right? You ran out on her! What kind of evil, horrible father does that? How could—?'

I knew I was shouting, and I didn't care.

Jenny put her hand on my arm. 'Being angry isn't really going to help Kate,' she said. 'Why don't you just explain to Patrick exactly why you're here?'

I knew she was right, so I took a few deep breaths and tried to calm myself. Ruby squeezed my hand, almost like by doing so she could give me some of her strength.

Even so, I knew already that it wasn't going to work. Patrick had moved on, and there was no room for Kate in his cosy new life.

Still, though, I owed it to Kate to try, so, in a cold voice, I told Patrick all about Martha – his own mother – getting sick. He looked worried for a second, but relaxed when I said that all she needed was a few months' rest. Then I went on to tell him about the social workers and the foster care and everything.

'Poor Kate,' he said when I was finished. 'My poor, poor little girl.'

He spoke so gently that, for one moment, I dared to think that there might be some hope.

'Kate doesn't want to live with a foster family,' I said. 'She wants to stay in her own home, and you're the only one who can make that happen. You need to go back to Seacove and stay there with her. It'll only be for a few months. After that, Martha will be better, so you can leave if you want to. But you probably won't want to, once you get to know Kate again. She's amazing. She's smart and funny and—'

Just then the sound of the baby's crying drifted towards us from the back of the house. Patrick turned and looked over his shoulder nervously, and suddenly I understood.

'Zoe knows nothing about your life in Ireland, does she?' I said. 'I bet she doesn't even know that Kate exists.'

Patrick didn't reply, but his guilty face told me all I needed to know.

I felt like shoving past him and running in to tell Zoe the truth.

Why did she deserve to live happily ever after while poor Kate had so little?

Once again Jenny read my mind.

'Let it go, Eva,' she said. 'It's not your secret to tell. And none of this is Zoe's fault anyway.'

I knew she was right. I forced myself to forget about Zoe and baby Simon, and I glared at Patrick.

'Kate is your daughter. What are you going to do to help her?'

Suddenly he looked old and weary.

'It's not easy,' he said. 'I can't just walk away from my family.'

'Why not?' I said, angry again. 'You did it once before.'

He flinched, almost like I'd hit him.

'And that's exactly why I can't do it again,' he said. 'I'm not a monster. I know how much I must have hurt Kate, so I can't do the same to anyone else.'

'But what about Kate? She hasn't gone away. She needs you. You can't just ignore that.'

'I'm starting a new job soon,' he said. 'And things won't be so tight financially. I'll be able to send Kate some money.'

'Money!' I almost spat the word at him. 'She needs more than money. She needs a father.'

'You're young,' he said. 'You don't understand yet just how complicated things can get when you are older. You see—'

'I can see one thing very clearly,' I said. 'And it's that I'm wasting my time. We're leaving – and don't worry, your secret is safe with me. I won't tell Kate about your new family. It would hurt her too much, and she sooo doesn't deserve that.'

As I walked down the short driveway, Ruby and Jenny walked beside me, like bodyguards.

Then when I got to the gate, I stopped and looked back. I realised that I absolutely didn't need bodyguards. Patrick was leaning against the doorway, looking sad and old and defeated.

A kinder person than me might have felt sorry for him, but I needed all my sympathy for Kate.

'Know what?' I shouted back at him. 'Kate's much better off without you.'

He looked ashamed, but still he turned and went inside, closing the door firmly behind him.

✮ ♛ ♡

That evening, Andrea brought us to a park near Jenny's flat. He spread a huge rug on the grass, and Jenny, Ruby and I stretched ourselves out in the still-warm sunshine.

'Don't go away,' he said. 'I'll be back in twenty minutes.'

Jenny turned to me. 'I'm sorry things didn't turn out better today, Eva,' she said.

'Me too,' I said.

'But you did your best, so don't feel bad. And now you should try to enjoy your last evening in London.'

I knew she was right, but I wasn't sure I could take her advice. Was it fair of me to enjoy anything, when my friend's life was such a mess?

Then Andrea came back carrying a huge wicker basket and a guitar.

'All my grandmother's favourite recipes,' he said, as he unpacked tubs of pasta and salad and warm garlic bread.

We ate until every scrap was finished, and then Andrea started to play his guitar. A young couple sat down near us, and the girl started to sing along to Andrea's music, and I lay in the sunshine and thought that this had to be the best place in the whole world.

Much later, when we were packing up to go home, Andrea dragged Ruby over to the couple.

'This is Ruby Miller,' he said. 'You don't know her yet, but one day she is going to be a champion swimmer. Maybe you should get her autograph now, before the rush.'

Everyone laughed and Ruby went totally red, but she was smiling too.

'Andrea's lovely,' I whispered to Jenny.

'I know,' she said, with a dreamy look on her face.

'What am I missing?' asked Andrea coming over.

'Oh, just a family secret,' said Jenny, and she gave me a big long hug.

Chapter Eighteen

When we walked through the arrivals area the next morning, Ruby covered her eyes.

'OMG!' she said.

I looked through the glass door to see Mum and Ruby's mum waiting for us. Maggie was waving a beautiful hand-stitched flag. *WELL DONE, RUBY!* it said, in shiny gold letters. On her shirt she was wearing a huge badge that said *My Daughter is a Swimming Star.*

'How totally embarrassing is that?' asked Ruby.

I giggled. 'She's just proud of you.'

'Well, I wish she could be proud of me in a more subtle way,' she said.

We walked through the doors, and spent ages hugging and kissing and talking about the swimming trials.

'You will never know just how proud you have made me, Ruby,' said Maggie after a while.

Ruby looked at me and I knew what she was thinking.

I shook my head – there was no need for Maggie to know the finer points of what had happened at the swimming trial. But Ruby has a stubborn, honest streak.

'I nearly didn't get the scholarship,' she said. 'I nearly threw it all away at the last minute.'

The smile faded from Maggie's face. 'What happened?' she asked.

Before Ruby could answer, I spoke for her.

'She just got a bit nervous, that's all. It wasn't a big deal.'

'It *was* a big deal,' said Ruby. 'It was a *very* big

deal. My swimming trial was a total disaster.'

'But you still got through, didn't you?' asked Maggie.

'Yes, but only because of Eva,' said Ruby. 'She was totally brilliant. She talked to me and then she talked to the coach and persuaded her to give me another chance. If it weren't for Eva, I would never, ever have got the scholarship.'

I looked at Maggie, and felt a sudden flash of pity. She was going to be so lonely when Ruby packed up and left for London. On long, dark winter nights, was she going to hate me?

Even though I'd done exactly as she asked?

But then Maggie beamed and stretched up and hugged me. It was almost like she could read my mind.

'I'm going to miss Ruby so much,' she said. 'But missing her is nothing compared to how proud I am of her. I am so very happy that she's got this wonderful opportunity. Thank you, Eva. You are quite simply amazing.'

Her words made me embarrassed at first, and then, as the embarrassment faded, I began to feel cross.

If I was so amazing, how come I couldn't do a single thing to help Kate?

☼ ★ ♡

Mum dropped Maggie and Ruby home, and then we continued our journey to Seacove.

'Kate's going to visit a possible foster family tomorrow,' said Mum as we drove.

'Poor Kate,' I said. 'I bet it's going to be like an *X-Factor* audition. How long does she get to impress the family? If they don't like what they see, do they get to say mean stuff about her? Do they tell her to go home and try again next year?'

'You're just being silly, Eva,' said Mum. 'You know it's not like that. Nicola and Tom have worked very hard to find a lovely family that will welcome Kate. I'm quite sure they'll do everything they can to make her happy.'

I knew Mum was right, but that didn't stop me from feeling terribly sorry for Kate.

'How is she?' I asked, not sure I wanted to hear the answer.

'Oh, you know,' said Mum in the end. 'Kate's busy being Kate.'

And then, before I could stop myself, I told Mum the story of the search for Kate's dad, and what a total waste of time the whole thing had been.

When I stopped talking, Mum was strangely quiet. I looked across and saw that her eyes were glistening with tears.

'Eva, that's so sweet of you,' she said.

'Yeah, sweet and useless,' I said. 'I didn't achieve anything.'

'But you tried,' said Mum. 'You did your best and that's what counts.'

'It doesn't do anything to help Kate, though, does it?'

Mum sighed. 'Sometimes problems are just too big, Eva. Sometimes there's nothing at all you can do.'

That was a really horrible thought, so I turned up the radio, closed my eyes and tried not to dread meeting Kate again.

❀ ★ ♡

When we got to the house, Kate came out to meet us. She was wearing a really nice top, and new jeans that Mum had bought for her. Mum had taken her to the hairdressers too, so her hair had a really cool cut.

'You look great,' I said. 'And Mum says you're going to see a family tomorrow.

Kate smiled at me, but it was an empty, brittle smile, like the last pathetic spark in a dying fire.

'Let's not talk about that now,' she said. 'Tell me all about London instead. I want to hear every single detail.'

That immediately set up a barrier between us.

How could I tell her every single detail of my trip?

How could I tell her about my stupid, stupid search for her stupid, stupid dad?

So I told her all about Ruby and the swimming trials, and the fun we'd had with Jenny, and about how cute and nice Andrea was.

And all the time I was talking, I had the horrible, weird fear that I was somehow going to blurt out the awful truth – *I met your dad, and he rejected you all over again.*

Chapter Nineteen

Next morning I helped Kate to get ready for her meeting with the foster family.

'You should wear your new jeans,' I said. 'And I can lend you that green top you've always liked.'

Kate put on the clothes and looked at herself critically in the mirror.

'I feel like I'm going on trial. It's like an *X-Factor* audition or something.'

'That's totally ridiculous,' I said, like I hadn't already thought the exact same thing. 'Anyway, if anyone is going to be on trial today, it has to be the family. You're trying them out to see if *they're* good enough for *you*.'

'But—'

I didn't let her finish. 'You're an amazing girl, Kate,' I said. 'And this family will be very lucky if you agree to live with them.'

Suddenly Kate ran from the room. When she came back a few minutes later, she had messed up her hair, and she was wearing one of her old tracksuits that looked crumpled and dirty.

She sat on the bed and folded her arms defiantly.

'I might not have a choice,' she said. 'But the family will. If I make them hate me, they won't take me, and that will be the end of that.'

'But that's not a solution. You have to live somewhere – there's no way you'll be allowed to stay on your own, and we're leaving next week, and …'

I stopped talking when I saw that tears were rolling down Kate's face. I ran over and hugged her for a long time.

Finally she pulled away, and gazed at me with the saddest eyes I'd ever seen.

I tried to smile. 'It'll be fine, Kate,' I said. 'Nicola told Mum that the family you're meeting today is really nice. They're called the Dalys. They have heaps of pets – and you like animals, so that's all good. And anyway, in a few months time, Martha will be well enough to come home, and then everything will be fine again. Try and be brave, Kate, please.'

'Sure,' said Kate, wiping her eyes. 'I can do brave – after all, I've had plenty of practice.'

❀ ♥ ✧

By the time Tom and Nicola arrived to bring Kate to meet the Dalys, she had changed back into the nice clothes, and fixed her hair. She'd washed her face, and her eyes were only slightly red.

'All set?' asked Tom as we stood at the door.

Kate just stared at him, and didn't answer.

'I know you're nervous,' said Nicola. 'And that's understandable, but Tom and I will do all we can to make things easy for you.'

Still Kate said nothing.

'The Dalys live only a few miles from here,' said Tom. 'You'll still be able to hang out with your friends and, after the holidays, you can go back to your own school.'

'You can bring all your own things with you, so it won't feel too strange,' said Nicola.

'And we'll arrange for you to visit Martha too,' added Tom.

It was like they were both competing, to see who'd be the first to make Kate smile. I could have warned them that they were wasting their time. When Kate's decided to sulk, nothing will make her change her mind.

Tom and Nicola walked towards the car.

I hugged Kate.

'It'll be fine,' I said. 'Trust me.'

And then I wondered why she should possibly

trust me since I'd gone behind her back and then failed miserably in my attempt to help her.

❋　♥　☼

Two hours later, Kate was back. Nicola and Tom went to talk to Mum and Dad, and Kate sat outside in the garden with me. Her face had the blank, secretive look that I remembered from the summer before.

'So how did it go?' I asked. 'What was the family like?'

'It went fine and the family was fine,' said Kate.

Over the next twenty minutes, I tried lots of different questions, but I didn't get any more information. Talking to Kate was like shouting into a cave. My own questions came bouncing back, just ever-so-slightly changed. I did my best, but I was kind of relieved when Kate said she wanted to go inside and be on her own for a while.

When Nicola and Tom left, Mum came out to the garden. 'It's all sorted,' she said. 'Nicola has to do some paperwork, but that won't take long. As soon as it's finished, Kate can move in with the Dalys.'

'But that's so sad,' I said.

Mum sighed. 'I know it seems that way right now, Eva, but it's the best possible solution. The Dalys are a really lovely family, and they're very much looking forward to having Kate stay with them.'

I thought of Kate's sullen face, and her almost rude answers. I knew the real Kate, but if I didn't I'm not sure I'd be happy at the thought of looking at that sulky expression all day long.

Mum must have read my mind. 'Foster families get a lot of training. They'll understand why Kate is upset.'

'You're sure?'

'Sure I'm sure. Remember what Kate was like last year, but you still managed to see through to the lovely girl underneath. They'll work it out. Just you wait and see.'

★ ❀ ☾

A few days later, Kate was ready to leave. When her bags were packed and waiting in the hall, there was still an hour to go until Nicola was due to pick her up.

We stood and looked at each other, and I wondered desperately how we were going to pass the long minutes.

In the end, Mum came to the rescue.

'Why don't you go and call for Lily?' she asked.

I totally wished that I could.

'She's gone to visit her cousins in Dublin,' I said.

'Well, looking at each other with long faces isn't helping anyone,' said Mum. 'You two had better go somewhere and do something, or I'll have to ask you to do the ironing.'

Kate and I both hate ironing, so there was no need for discussion.

'We're going,' I said, as I raced towards the door with Kate following close behind me.

When we got outside, we looked at each other again.

'Come on,' said Kate with a sigh. 'Let's go say goodbye to Jeremy.'

I followed her along the familiar road to her favourite field and her favourite tree. Kate flung herself on to the grass, and I lay beside her. For a while we lay in silence, watching the leaves rustling over our heads.

It was hard to know what to say.

I'd already said 'it'll be fine' a million times.

And a million times, Kate had shrugged and not answered, almost like she didn't care anyway.

Suddenly Kate sat up and stared at me.

'Last year,' she said.

'Last year what?'

'Last year, when the developers were

threatening to cut Jeremy down, there didn't seem to be any hope of saving him. But you found a way, Eva. Against all the odds, you found a way to save Jeremy.'

'It wasn't just me,' I said, embarrassed. 'It was you, and my parents, and Martha and Lily and the locals, and the tourists and …'

'But it was mostly you,' she said. 'It was amazing. It was just like magic. So …'

'So what?'

Now she looked embarrassed too. 'Now I need you to work your magic again. The Dalys are a nice family, but I don't want to live with strangers. I just want to stay here until Martha gets better, and you're the only one who can help me. Please, Eva, can't you think of anything?'

I looked at her and thought I was going to die of sadness. Apart from stupid, hopeless plans of running away, I couldn't think of a single thing to help her.

'I'm so sorry, Kate.' I said. 'I'm all out of

amazing magic plans.'

She shrugged and tried to smile. 'That's OK,' she said.

Then I knew the time had come to be honest. 'There's another thing too, Kate,' I said, as I sat up. 'But if I say it, you might hate me.'

'But you're my best friend. I'd never hate you.'

I wasn't so sure, but I couldn't pretend any more.

'I don't want to help you.' An angry look flashed across her face, but I knew I had to continue. 'What I mean is, I *do* want to help you, but if I did, I'd be doing the wrong thing. You see, I know you're scared of going to live with the Daly's – and that's perfectly normal. I'd feel the same.'

'But?' Her face was blank again.

'But living with the Dalys is going to be a million times better than staying on your own. I couldn't bear for you to spend another single night inside that dark and empty house. So, even if I came up with the most amazing escape plan in the world, I wouldn't share it with you.'

Kate was quiet for a long time. I lay down again and gazed up at the rustling leaves. I wondered if I'd managed to ruin our friendship forever.

Then, after ages and ages, she spoke in a quiet voice.

'Thank you for being honest,' she said.

I felt sick. If I was so honest, how come I couldn't mention the small detail of her dad's new wife and their totally sweet new baby?

❀　☼　❀

An hour later, I watched the back of Kate's head, as Nicola drove her away to her new home.

'Why isn't she waving?' asked Joey. 'Has she forgotten about us already?'

'No,' said Mum, patting his head. 'She hasn't forgotten us. She's probably just excited.'

Joey was satisfied with that explanation, but I

knew Mum hadn't been telling the truth. Kate was too proud to let us see her tears.

'Bye, Kate,' I whispered, and then I went to my room and stared at the ceiling for a very long time.

Chapter Twenty

The next few days were weird. Lily was still away visiting her cousins and without her and Kate, Seacove was just a boring village by the sea. A few times I was so fed up I even volunteered to play Monopoly with Joey.

Then, on the last night of my holidays, Ruby came to stay over, and I was totally glad to see her.

'I'm so glad you invited me,' she said. 'I leave for London in a few days, and I wanted to see you before I go.'

'Are you excited?'

'Yeah, excited and a bit scared. Mostly excited

though. I know it's going to be amazing, and if it weren't for you, it wouldn't be happening.'

'Well I'm glad I was able to help someone,' I said.

'How's Kate?' asked Ruby, guessing what I was thinking of.

I told her all about the foster family.

'So basically, I wasted your time in London,' I said. 'I didn't manage to change anything.'

'But you did your best,' she said. 'And that means something.'

'Does it?'

She nodded. 'And besides, foster care isn't so bad.'

Something in her voice made me look up.

'You sound like you know that from personal experience.'

'When Mum had her accident, she was in hospital for months, and there was no one to mind me and Jenny, so ...'

'But you never said.

She giggled. 'You never asked.'

'So what was it like?'

She shrugged. 'It was OK. I missed Mum and our house like crazy, but the foster family was really nice. I still visit them sometimes. Kate will be fine, you'll see.'

'I just wish I knew that for sure. I have no way of contacting her until I get the Dalys' phone number and …'

Just then my phone rang.

'It's an unknown number,' I said. 'It's probably Joey and some of his friends playing one of their not-funny tricks.'

But it was Kate.

'It's so good to hear from you,' I said. 'Whose phone are you using?'

'It's mine. Joan and Denis bought it for me.'

'Joan and Denis?'

'The Dalys.'

I grinned. If *The Dalys* had turned into *Joan and Denis* already, that had to be good news.

'Anyway,' she said. 'What time are you leaving tomorrow? Joan and Denis said they'll bring me to Seacove to pick up a few things from home, and if you're still there, we can hang out for a bit.'

'We're not going till after lunch.'

'Perfect. See you at eleven then.'

And before I could say any more, she hung up.

☺ ♥ ✽

Ruby left early the next morning, and I waited very impatiently for Kate.

When she arrived, we hugged for a long time. Then I stepped away and looked at her.

She wasn't fully back to normal, but her eyes were a bit brighter, and I could see tiny traces of the clever, funny girl I'd known the year before.

'Let's go visit Jeremy,' she said. 'He'll be really surprised to see me again so soon.'

A few minutes later, we were lying on our

usual spot under the tree.

'So tell me everything,' I said.

'What's to tell? Joan and Denis are really nice, and their house is totally cool. It's kind of like a mini-zoo. They've got three dogs, four cats, heaps of birds and even a pet donkey.'

'That sounds good.'

'Sometimes it's still a bit weird. When I wake up in the mornings, I forget for a minute where I am – and when I remember, it's ...'

'It's what?'

'I don't know really. Joan and Denis couldn't be kinder but ... it's just ... it's just that I don't feel like I'm really at home there.'

'How do you mean?'

'I feel like I've got to be polite all the time. I'm never sure if it's OK to wander around in my pyjamas, or if Joan and Denis are going to get mad at me if I lie on the couch watching tv all afternoon.'

'That sounds kind of normal to me.'

'Does it?'

I nodded. 'And remember,' I said. 'You've only been there for a few days. It's going to take you a while to settle in properly.'

'You think so?'

'I know so.'

She smiled. 'You're probably right – anyway, every day is a little bit less strange than the one that went before.'

'So you're happy?'

She hesitated for so long before answering, that I had to turn to see if she'd fallen asleep or run away or something.

'Happy's a big word,' she said slowly. 'It's like you predicted all the time. Everything's fine.'

But was fine the best Kate could hope for?

Stories are supposed to end with the heroine living happily ever after.

Was sort-of-happy-ever-after good enough?

✧　☼　❀

Later we walked back home.

'Mum's making pancakes,' I said. 'Denis and Joan aren't coming until four, so you'll have plenty of time to eat some.'

'Yum,' said Kate. 'But first I need to pick up some stuff from my place.'

'Sure,' I said, following her.

Then she stopped, embarrassed. 'I'd kind of like to go on my own,' she said.

'Sure,' I said again. 'I'll wait here.'

It was nice sitting on the wall in the sunshine, listening to the birds singing in the hedges.

Then the sound of a car coming along the lane, ruined the peace.

'That so isn't fair,' I muttered, convinced that it was Denis and Joan back too early.

But then the car came closer, and I could see that the only occupant was a man – a familiar man.

But it couldn't be.

Or could it?

The car came even closer, and at last I could see for sure.

It was Kate's dad, Patrick.

Chapter Twenty-One

'O-mi-god,' I breathed as the car stopped and Patrick climbed out.

'You again,' he said, and I couldn't tell if he was glad or sad to see me.

I looked desperately towards Kate's house, but there was no sign of her.

I didn't know if I wanted her to appear or not.

'I suppose you're surprised to see me,' said Patrick.

'Of course I'm surprised,' I said coolly. 'You said you weren't coming. You said—'

'I said a lot of things, and most of them were rubbish.'

'I can't argue with that,' I said.

'Anyway, I'm here now.'

Suddenly I had a horrible thought.

'Hey,' I said sharply. 'If you're thinking of hanging out with Kate for an afternoon, and then running out on her again, that sooo isn't a good idea.'

'But—'

I know it's rude to interrupt adults, but I didn't let that small detail stop me, 'Kate's moved in with a foster family,' I said. 'She's trying really hard to make it work. If you march into her life for a few hours, and mess everything up, that would be a disaster. You can't do it to her. It wouldn't be fair.'

Patrick raised one eyebrow. 'Are you telling me what to do?'

Suddenly I felt really brave.

'Yes,' I said. 'Actually, I *am* telling you what to do. Kate's my friend, and I won't let you hurt her all over again.'

Now he looked old and sad.

'You were right, you know,' he said.

'About what?'

'Zoe knew nothing about Kate. I know that was wrong, but somehow, I'd never found the right time to tell her. After talking to you, though, I knew I couldn't live a lie any more. So I told her everything.'

'And?'

'And she was really mad at me for a while, but once she got over that, she started to think about finding a way to help Kate.'

'And?'

'And my new job is as a journalist for an environmental magazine. It's a job I can do from pretty much anywhere. And Zoe's taken time out from her career to be with Simon, so the three of us are going to move back here with Kate. We're going to start over. That's if ...'

'If what?'

Now he looked even older and sadder than before.

'If Kate can ever forgive me.'

'That's a big "if",' I said. 'Kate's the most stubborn girl I've ever met.'

For the first time he smiled. 'Good,' he said. 'That's exactly how I remember her.'

❤   ☀   ♡

The sound of Kate's front door slamming made us both jump.

'Hey, Eva,' called Kate from over the hedge, 'can you come and give me a hand please? This bag is huge, and really heavy.'

'Sorry,' I said. 'I'm kind of busy, but I'll send someone else, OK?'

'Whatever. Just hurry before my back breaks.'

Patrick looked like he had turned to stone, so I shook his arm.

'Didn't you hear that?' I asked. 'I think your daughter needs you.'

He took a deep, shaky breath and started to walk. I followed him as far as the gap in the hedge. He stopped walking when he saw Kate standing on the doorstep of the house.

Kate looked up and saw him.

There was a very long silence, and I had to bite my tongue to stop myself saying something stupid.

Finally Patrick spoke two strangled, choked words.

'My Kate.'

Kate spoke a single, equally strangled word.

'Dad?'

Patrick walked slowly towards her, and as he walked, I watched the expression on Kate's face change from surprise to joy to anger and back to surprise again. She folded her arms, and stared at her father, watching his every move. She didn't turn away, though – not for a single fraction of a second. I knew that was a good sign.

I turned around and walked home.

I was beginning to think that maybe this story was going to have a happy ending after all.

Chapter Twenty-Two

*A*nd that was pretty much that.

As soon as I got home from Seacove I called over to Victoria's place.

'So how was California?' I asked, as soon as we'd finished hugging. 'Was it really as good as you said in all those texts?'

'It was totally brilliant,' she said. 'And how was Seacove?'

I hesitated, and she looked a bit embarrassed. Then I grinned. 'Funnily enough,' I said, 'Seacove was totally brilliant too.'

A few weeks later, I was settled back at school, and it was almost like all the crazy stuff with Ruby and Kate had never happened.

And then one day I got *two* letters.

The first was from Ruby:

Hi Eva,

I know this is the twenty-first century, but my ancient English teacher has insisted that we all write a letter today – so I've decided to write to you. This place is great. I'm sharing a room with a girl called Asmita – she's really nice – and so are most of the other kids here. Mrs Armitage is still the scariest person I've ever met, but she's ok underneath – I think.

She often asks me about you – which I think is totally weird!

We swim every single morning and evening. One weekend I was allowed to go and stay with Jenny. She says 'hi'. (And Andrea says 'ciao'.) Class is nearly over so I'd better finish.

Looking forward to seeing you at Christmas.

Your friend,
Ruby
Xxxx

PS If it weren't for you, I wouldn't be here. You're amazing!!

♔ ❧ ♥

The next letter was from Kate.

HEY, EVA!

HOW ARE THINGS?
I KNOW IT'S THE TWENTY-FIRST CENTURY, AND I HAVE A PHONE NOW, (JOAN AND DENIS LET ME KEEP IT) BUT I GOT USED TO WRITING TO YOU LAST YEAR, SO...
THINGS ARE GOOD HERE. ZOE IS TOTALLY GREAT. SHE DOESN'T TRY TO BE A MUM, WHICH IS A HUGE RELIEF - SHE'S

MORE LIKE A COOL BIG SISTER.

SIMON IS ACTUALLY THE SWEETEST BABY EVER. HE CALLS ME KAY-KAY WHICH IS ADORABLE.

DAD AND I ARE SLOWLY GETTING USED TO EACH OTHER. SOMETIMES WE HAVE THE WORST ROWS EVER. ZOE JUST LAUGHS AND SAYS IT'S BECAUSE I NEVER HAD A CHANCE TO BE A PROPER TEENAGER BEFORE.

MARTHA'S GETTING A LOT STRONGER AND THE DOCTORS SAY SHE'LL BE ABLE TO COME HOME AFTER CHRISTMAS. DAD'S SAVING UP TO BUILD AN EXTENSION SO THERE WILL BE ROOM FOR US ALL.

DAD AND ZOE AND SIMON HAD TO GO BACK TO LONDON FOR A FEW DAYS LAST WEEK. THEY ASKED ME TO GO WITH THEM BUT I SAID NO. I DIDN'T WANT TO MISS SCHOOL — SO I STAYED WITH JOAN AND DENIS. THEY'RE REALLY NICE — BUT I GUESS YOU'D FIGURED THAT OUT ALREADY.

ANYWAY, I'D BETTER GO. I PROMISED TO MIND SIMON FOR A WHILE SO DAD AND ZOE CAN GO FOR A WALK.

LOVE FROM KATE

PS DAD TOLD ME ABOUT YOU GOING TO SEE HIM IN LONDON.

THAT WAS TOTALLY CRAZY, BUT PROBABLY THE BEST THING
YOU EVER DID IN YOUR WHOLE LIFE. THANK YOU SO MUCH,
EVA - YOU'RE AMAZING.

And even though I don't feel the slightest bit
amazing, I do have a confession to make – that
night I went to bed with a huge smile on my
face!

The 'Eva' Series

by

Judi Curtin

Don't miss the other great books about Eva and her friends

Have you read them all?

Eva's Journey

Eva's Holiday

Leave it to Eva

Available from all good bookshops.

Eva Gordon is a
bit of a princess ...

But when her dad loses his job and she has to move
house and change schools, she realises things have changed
forever. A chance visit to a fortune teller gives her the idea
that doing good may help her to turn things back the way
they were. Eva (with the help of best friend Victoria) starts
to help everyone she can — whether they want it or not! And
maybe being nice is helping Eva herself just as much ...

**The story of
Eva's marvellous,
memorable summer!**

Eva Gordon likes fashion, fun and hanging out with friends,
so she can't believe she has to spend the entire summer in a
cottage in the countryside with her parents.

Worse, it looks like she's going to be stuck with Kate, the
girl next door who doesn't care about being cool ... But when
the girls have to pull together to solve a problem, Eva finds out
that there's more to life than having the right hair or clothes
and sometimes 'weird' girls can make the best friends.

THE 'ALICE & MEGAN' SERIES
BY

Judi Curtin

HAVE YOU READ THEM ALL?

Don't miss all the great books about Alice & Megan:

Alice Next Door
Alice Again
Don't Ask Alice
Alice in the Middle
Bonjour Alice
Alice & Megan Forever
Alice to the Rescue
Alice & Megan's Cookbook

Available from all good bookshops